feel THE fire

feel THE fire

ADRIANNE BYRD

ARABESQUE®

FEEL THE FIRE

An Arabesque novel

ISBN-13: 978-0-373-83022-0
ISBN-10:   0-373-83022-X

www.kimanipress.com

Printed in U.S.A.

Acknowledgment

To my family and friends, thanks for all the support and love that you've given me. To my editor, Evette Porter, thanks for lovin' my stories. To my wonderful fans and readers, thank you for allowing me to do what I do. It's always a pleasure to entertain you.

I wish you all the best of love,

Adrianne

Prologue

It was going to be a beautiful wedding.

Too bad thirteen-year-old Alyssa Jansen was going to miss it. Being the daughter of the hired help meant a lot of things, but it didn't mean one was automatically invited to the social event of the year.

Far from it.

However, she could still enjoy the magic drifting in the air. Weddings inspired such hope and wonderment about the future and this one had Alyssa dreaming about her own.

One day Quentin and I will walk down the aisle.

Sighing dreamily, Alyssa twirled around with her

arms stretched high above her head. Quentin Dwayne Hinton, her real-life Prince Charming. True, all the Hinton men were handsome. But Quentin had something extra special.

Dizzy, she giggled aloud and then bumped into her father. "Oh," she gasped. "Sorry, Dad. I didn't see you."

Alfred Jansen, Roger Hinton's personal chef, was a six-foot-four robust man with a long, silver mane of hair and matching goatee that made him look more like a mountain lion than a man. His commanding presence immediately garnered respect and he certainly ran the Hintons' kitchens with an iron hand. But underneath, everyone knew this lion was nothing but a kitten at heart.

"Alyssa, honey. You have to get out of the way. We're trying to get ready for the wedding." Alfred smiled despite the reprimand. He'd always found it difficult to scold his daughter and everyone knew it.

"I'm sorry, Dad. I'll get out of the way."

The florist and her assistants rushed around the father and daughter, setting up the arrangements, while one guy ran past with a cage of doves.

"Oh, Daddy, look. They're going to release birds."

"Uh-huh." He grabbed her by the hand. "Too bad you're going to miss it."

Alyssa poked out her bottom lip. Why did he have to remind her?

"Do me a favor," her father said, directing her back toward the kitchen. "Stay out of the trees."

"What?" she asked, horrified. She was a natural monkey when it came to climbing and she already had her mind set on perching in her favorite Southern red oak tree with her binoculars and a bag of Cheetos. "But I wanted to see the wedding."

"You can listen to it from your bedroom."

"Listen to it? That's not the same thing. One doesn't *listen* to a wedding. You *see* a wedding. You *experience* it."

Her father shook his head and remained firm. "You fell out of that large oak last week and almost experienced a broken neck," he reminded her. "Case you haven't noticed, I have enough to worry about around here. Like trying to feed twelve hundred guests."

Alyssa clamped her mouth shut.

"Promise me," he said.

She groaned, wishing he hadn't added that. What girl could resist watching a fairy-tale wedding in her own backyard? Didn't he know he was asking the impossible?

"Ally." He stopped and spun her around by the shoulders. "Promise me," he insisted.

Alyssa sighed and dropped her head. "I promise," she mumbled to her feet, but kept her fingers crossed behind her back.

"Hmm. Something smells wonderful in here."

Alyssa and Alfred turned to see Quentin enter the kitchen and make a beeline toward one of the long silver trays.

Alyssa froze.

Quentin, Q as his friends called him, wasn't as tall as her father; but at six foot two, lean, and with a beautiful butterscotch complexion, it was no wonder why women practically drooled whenever he was around.

Alyssa included.

"What's in here, Alfred?" Q asked, lifting a tray cover.

"Ah, ah, ah. Master Quentin. Those lobster pot stickers are for the wedding."

Q quickly swiped one and plopped it in his mouth with a wink.

Alyssa stifled a giggle at his playful antics.

"Mr. Hinton, please," her father begged. "Everything must be perfect or Sterling will have my head on one of these silver platters."

When Q laughed, Alyssa thought it was the most beautiful sound on earth.

"Oh, loosen up, Alfred. Knowing you, everything will be *more* than 'perfect.' Relax. Personally, I can't believe Jonas is crazy enough to give this whole marriage thing another try. Who knows? This time we might even reach the 'I do' part." Q laughed heartily and to Alyssa's amazement, his eyes landed on her.

"Oh, hello, Alice." He headed toward her.

Alyssa's eyes bugged and her tongue glued itself to the roof of her mouth.

"My, my. Aren't you a tall weed?" He looked her over. "How old are you now?"

She blinked while her mind went blank beneath his twinkling brown eyes.

After a lengthy silence, Quentin frowned. "Alfred, I think there's something wrong with your daughter. She's not a mute, is she?"

"No...um. She's shy."

"Oh." His gaze raked over her bony legs, flat chest and large eyes. "You better watch out for this one," he told Alfred. "She's going to break plenty of hearts when she grows up." He tweaked her right cheek. "Mine included," he added for her ears only.

Never!

"Don't I know it." Her father winked at her from over Q's shoulder, oblivious to the youngest Hinton's teasing.

"There you are!" Sterling Hinton burst into the kitchen. "I've been looking all over the place for you."

Quentin swung his arm around Alyssa's shoulders before turning to face his older brother. "You know me, I can't stand to be apart from beautiful women."

Alyssa's face flushed with heat. *His arm is around my shoulder!*

"Don't you think Alyssa is a little *too* young for you?"

She frowned at Sterling. Who was he to come rain on her parade?

"First of all," Q said, waving a finger. "Her name is *Alice.* Second of all... Well, there's no second."

"Have you been drinking?" Sterling asked, suspiciously.

"There's no law against it and it's well past noon. At least five minutes or so."

Fire lit behind Sterling's eyes and Alyssa cowered. Sterling didn't explode often; but when he did, watch out.

"If you ruin this day for Jonas," Sterling seethed,

jabbing a finger into the center of Q's chest. "I swear, I'll kill you."

Q's arms fell from Alyssa's shoulders as he smiled in an attempt to tame a dragon. "I resent that. I was on my best behavior at Jonas's last wedding and I will be so again tonight. *But* if there's a third one, all bets are off."

"Smart-ass."

"Hey, hey. Watch the language in front of young Alice." Q looped his arm around his brother and directed him out of the kitchen. "The poor girl is painfully shy."

When the Hinton brothers disappeared out of the kitchen, Alyssa's small shoulders slumped forward as her tongue finally unglued itself. "My name isn't Alice."

"Tough break, sweetheart." Her father tugged her fat pigtail. "At least this time he paid you a compliment."

"Some compliment."

"He basically said one day you'll be so beautiful you'll have your pick of any man, if my heart can take it, and the ones you don't choose will be heartbroken."

"Then I choose Quentin."

"Who knows? Maybe one day you'll have him." He sighed. "But you should keep your options open. Wide-open."

Alyssa knew her father didn't approve of Quentin, but he never came right out and discouraged her from her lofty claims to marry the man.

Mainly because Q was a playboy. Yes, she knew

what a playboy was. Thirteen didn't mean she was naive. Besides, it didn't matter. When she grew up, Q would only have eyes for her. She would make sure of it.

A line of servers bowled through the kitchen's swinging doors and nearly knocked Alyssa over.

Her father cocked his head and gave her a pleading look.

"I'm going. I'm going," Alyssa said dejectedly, and shuffled out of the kitchen with her head down. She headed out of the main house by the back door, hoping to catch one last look at the beautiful preparations.

Her frown drooped to an all-time low as she crept across the yard toward the servants' quarters. However, to get there, she had to pass her favorite oak tree. As she approached, a pair of male voices drifted on the afternoon air.

"Are you sure you're ready to do this again, son?"

Alyssa recognized her father's employer, Roger Hinton's, voice and she crouched down behind a line of shrubbery to eavesdrop.

"There won't be any surprises at this wedding, will there?"

"I can only hope not," Jonas joked with a nervous titter. "I think this time I picked someone who really wants to marry me."

"Good. Good," Mr. Hinton encouraged. "That's always a good strategy. Well, at any rate, I'm glad you chose to have the wedding here at the house. I can't tell you how much it means to your mother. Of course, she's hell-bent on getting the other two married off."

Jonas's gruff laughter rumbled around the men. "Good luck with Quentin. Mom might have to hogtie him and drag him down the aisle."

"True. The boy is as stubborn as a mule. He inherited that from your mother's side of the family."

Offended for her future husband, Alyssa rolled her eyes. There was no one more hardheaded than Roger Hinton. A man who built a real-estate empire by never accepting the word *no* and greasing a few pockets to make sure that he never would.

"You know, son. You never did tell me how you came to meet this new bride of yours."

"Didn't I?"

"No." A long puff of his cigar trailed his clipped answer and then, "There's even talk around the house that she dated Sterling for a minute."

Alyssa's eyes widened at that revelation.

"I didn't know you listened to idle gossip, Dad."

"I've always found there's a little truth to gossip and I have to say I'm mighty curious. Me *and* your mother. Who is she? Where did she come from? And please tell me you had the bride sign a prenuptial agreement this time around. There are rumors you don't like those things, as well."

Jonas chuckled. "I'm not going to answer the prenuptial question, Dad. But it is sort of an interesting story about how Toni and I met...."

Serendipity

Chapter 1

Then, Atlanta Hartsfield-Jackson Airport

Flight 1269 for Los Angeles was delayed. Toni Wright entered through the lobby doors of the cocktail lounge of the airline's Crown Room in desperate need of a drink. Instead her eyes zeroed in on a handsome brother at the bar who looked like he wanted to drown his sorrows in his glass.

Fleetingly, she wondered what could be so bad, but the last thing she wanted to do was play Dear Abby to some stranger. At the bar, she ordered a Cosmopolitan. As she waited, her gaze drifted back to the man.

He was tall, just like she liked them, and well

dressed. In fact, he had a certain aura of power and prestige. That was definitely a plus.

Toni wished he would look up so she could see his eyes. She had a feeling they were beautiful.

"Here you go, ma'am," the bartender said.

Toni smiled and laid down a tip. She turned to walk away but then felt compelled to make small talk with the brooding brother. Why not?

"A penny for your thoughts," she said, and then cringed at the campy line. When he didn't respond, she felt like an idiot. Never one to shy away from a challenge, Toni settled into the chair next to him.

It was a good thing, too; the man's heavenly fragrance was seductive enough to melt off a woman's panties.

He reached for his glass and drained the rest of his drink.

"Buy you another?" she asked.

Finally, he glanced her way. Just as she thought, he had beautiful eyes.

"I always thought that men were supposed to do the asking, not the other way around?"

Toni's toes curled at the velvety smoothness of his voice. "I figured we could make an exception, seeing how you look as if you needed it."

A corner of his lips curled and an adorable dimple appeared. "That's very kind of you, but—"

"And if it makes you feel better, you can buy my next one." She winked and flashed him her best smile.

He hesitated, looked her over and then nodded. "Deal."

While Toni signaled for the bartender, she could feel the man's eyes linger. She hoped he liked what he saw, but there were no guarantees, since she'd dressed down for travel.

"You're a lawyer," he said flatly.

Astonished, she glanced back at him. "How did you know that?"

He smiled again. "You have that look about you."

"Oh?" She crossed her arms. "And what look is that?"

"The I-can-eat-anyone-alive-and-still-have-room-for-dessert look."

She laughed and managed to maintain eye contact. "Does that look scare you?"

"Very little scares me." His smile diminished, but he remained polite.

"Another scotch on the rocks for the gentleman," the bartender announced.

For a few minutes after the drink was delivered, Toni found herself at a loss as to how to keep the conversation going. She had already used the penny-for-your-thoughts line, and she just wasn't willing to demean herself by asking for his zodiac sign.

"Thanks for the drink, but I don't think I'm going to be very good company," he said.

She considered him for a moment and warred with herself as to whether to stay or leave. "You know, I've been told I'm a pretty good listener," she said. "And it looks like I have plenty of time to kill."

"You don't want to hear my sob story."

She smiled. "Maybe I can help."

"Trust me. I've heard it all. Trouble don't last always. This, too, shall pass. Or my personal favorite—there are plenty of fish in the sea."

Genuine concern crept into her voice. "So someone broke your heart?"

"That's putting it mildly."

Toni drew a deep breath. "Who was she?"

"Someone…very special," he whispered. "Someone I loved the moment I laid eyes on her."

She waited for him to continue, but she saw she had to nudge a little more. "Does this woman have a name?"

He nodded. "Yes. Ophelia Missler. I guess you can say that it all started at a wedding…."

Toni remained true to her word and listened to the man's heartbreaking story about a love gone awry. There were parts that were funny, sweet and endearing. The only problem was that it was a love story that involved three people—one too many by her count.

A couple of hours into the story, Toni thanked the bartender for another round before settling her gaze back on the handsome man beside her.

"So far this sounds like one hell of a triangle."

"Sometimes love gives you more than you bargained for," he said despondently.

"So I've been told," she whispered, taking a sip of her drink and watching with concern how he downed his own.

"You've never been in love?" he asked.

The question threw her off guard. Toni had dated

many men—from all walks of life. Some men had showed her a good time, others had taught her life lessons and the rest she'd rather forget.

"I'm going to take that as a no." He chuckled.

"Well, it's not that I don't believe in love or anything," she said, "but I've never experienced a lightning bolt or stared into the depths of a man's eyes and felt beyond a shadow of a doubt that I'd met my soul mate." Toni laughed, but then she was crushed by a wave of disappointment. She had come close once, but close didn't count.

"Then consider yourself lucky," he mumbled.

She didn't feel lucky. While she was out leaping tall buildings in a single bound, most of her friends had settled down and started families. Meanwhile, she couldn't decide whether owning a dog was too much of a commitment.

And yet, she was okay with being single. Preferred it, really, when she considered the hell her parents' marriage was.

"Flight 2193 is now ready for boarding. Flight 2193."

Toni sighed. At this rate, she should have taken a taxi to Los Angeles. "So what happened?" she asked, reaching for her glass. "I have to admit I'm intrigued."

"And here I thought I was boring you."

"Not hardly." She nudged him. "Go on. I'm dying to know how this all played out."

He glanced at his watch and gave a half shrug. "All right. Let's see. What happened next?"

Toni huddled closer as her handsome stranger

continued his story: boy gets girl, boy gives girl an ultimatum to get rid of the other boy, but things start unraveling at the seams.

"I think you're purposely drawing this story out to keep me on pins and needles," Toni complained after another hour had rolled by. "When are we going to get to the wedding?" She gasped. "Wait. Was there even a wedding?"

The bartender approached. "Can I get you two anything else?"

"I'm good," she said.

Her handsome storyteller simply shook his head, and the bartender silently drifted away.

Toni glanced back at her companion with a million questions racing through her mind. His story had the makings of a soap opera. Did this Ophelia Missler really love her childhood friend, Solomon, or had Jonas, her current drinking partner, stolen her heart?

"You know, I really don't know why I'm running off at the mouth like this. My rehashing this story isn't going to change how things turned out."

Fearful she wouldn't hear the rest of the story, Toni carefully placed a hand against his arm. "Maybe not, but talking about things can be therapeutic."

His silence seemed to stretch for an eternity before he finally met her gaze. "I guess you want to hear the rest?"

Toni nodded and leaned in close. However, the wedding turned out to be a disaster with the bride marching down the aisle; but unable to say "I do," and leaving Jonas at the altar while the bride ran off to Las Vegas to marry Solomon.

"Flight 1269 to Los Angeles is now ready for boarding."

"Oh, that's me." Toni dabbed her eyes and then slid her purse strap over her shoulder before she glanced at Jonas again. She didn't quite know what to say to such a bittersweet love story, especially since he had gotten the short end of the stick. "It looks like I did a lousy job in cheering you up," she admitted.

Jonas's adorable dimples flashed. "I don't know about that. It felt good to finally talk about it. It's been a year, and Lord knows, my brothers, though well-intentioned, have been unsuccessful in getting me to open up." He met her gaze. "Looks like you *are* a good listener."

"A year, huh?" Toni's interest perked.

"Yeah. I heard Ophelia and Solomon had a beautiful girl last month. For the most part, I've been able to move on. I'm a little nostalgic because today would've been our one-year anniversary."

Toni nodded as she studied him. "You know, I bet she was right about you," she said. "One day you'll make some woman a wonderful husband."

She didn't know what possessed her to say that, but she meant it. Maybe it was something about his eyes. He had kind eyes, though now upon closer inspection and after hearing his sob story, she could see he was still very much a scarred man. Most likely, he had even thrown in the towel when it came to love.

Pity.

Then again, hadn't she done the same thing?

Jonas leaned back and crossed his arms while he studied her. "Is that right?"

A delicious warmth swept throughout Toni's body, and if she was standing, she was certain her knees would've buckled.

"Now boarding Flight 1269 to Los Angeles…"

Reluctantly, Toni stood from her bar stool. She reached into her purse and withdrew a business card. "If you're ever in Los Angeles, give me a call."

Still watching her, Jonas accepted the card. "I just might do that, Ms.…" He glanced at her name and a wide smile eased across his lips. "Ms. Wright."

"Until then." She winked, and then made sure she swished her hips in just the right way as she strolled out of the Crown Room.

Jonas enjoyed the view as he pocketed the card. "Until then, Ms. Wright."

Chapter 2

Jonas swore this would be the last time he would fly commercial. The airlines were always losing baggage, overbooking flights, delaying flights or just flat-out canceling them. It was a wonder how any of the companies managed to stay in business. Not to mention, first class wasn't what it used to be. The only thing it meant nowadays was that you'd get your drinks first.

In truth, the last thing he needed was a drink. How many did he have sitting in the Crown Room talking to the attractive attorney—four? Five? Hell, he'd lost count.

Settling into his seat and waving off the stewardess when she asked for his order, Jonas turned and glanced out of the window. How pathetic he must have sounded in that bar. A year later and he was still moaning about Ophelia.

He had tried everything he could think of to get over her. He'd even been desperate enough to take Q's advice and jump into bed with an extremely long line of faceless but curvaceous beauties. Sure, they gave him physical pleasure, but emotionally, he was still tangled in knots.

It was better than getting emotionally attached. Hell, he'd take pleasure over pain any day.

Then there were days when he wanted to track down Solomon Bassett and drag him into a dark alley and have an old-fashioned fistfight. But what would that solve?

It wasn't that he was still in love with Ophelia. He wasn't. It was just…he wanted to get even.

Jonas pulled Toni's business card out from his shirt pocket. For no particular reason, he just studied the stylish gold font promoting her as an associate partner of the law offices of Kaplan, Grey & Kaplan.

Maybe he hadn't been too pathetic. She did give him her card after all, but what would be the point? He hardly ever went out to the west coast and he wasn't interested in a long-distance relationship.

"Just two ships passing," he whispered under his breath, and tucked the card back into his shirt. "Miss?" He waved the stewardess back over to his seat. "I think I will have a drink."

Toni dreamed about a very naked Jonas Hinton during her five-hour flight back to Los Angeles. She pictured his entire body to be a smooth, even caramel glaze color, which would go perfect against her chocolate skin. Also in the dream, she had the brother bending in every direction imaginable and hitting all her hot spots.

Judging by the sheepish grins from the passengers around her when she woke, she guessed she had been talking in her sleep and had given everyone quite an earful. However, she exited the plane with her head held high and an extra pep in her step.

Toni had lived her whole life marching to a slightly different beat. She wasn't quite a wild child, but she was by no means a goody-two-shoes, either. She quite simply worked hard and played hard, too. When it came to men…well, they were like a box of chocolates. She never knew which one she was going to get.

As long as she kept replenishing the box, she was happy.

It was late when she finally made it home to her overpriced studio flat and she was more than ready to dive into her bed and get some real sleep. However, her ringing phone prevented her from fulfilling that wish.

"Hey, Maria," she answered without even looking at the caller ID.

"Well, thank heavens you're alive," Maria barked in her thick Spanish accent. "You don't know how to pick up the phone and call?"

"Sorry. I know I was supposed to come to your party, but my flight was delayed and I'm just walking through the door."

"You're just *now* getting home?" she questioned dubiously.

"Yes. I swear," Toni assured. "Next Botox party, I'm there." Toni loved Maria to death and she was a beautiful woman, but she hated how vigorously her girl fought aging. If Maria wasn't pumping silicon, collagen or Botox into her body, she was lasering, tucking and stretching her skin to the max. In the two years since Toni moved to Los Angeles, she noticed this behavior was the norm. California women were obsessed with youth.

Toni, once again, offered up a prayer of thanks for her good genes. Her skin was just as smooth and supple as any twenty-year-old's. Her casual workouts and active sex drive kept her curves tight and cellulite nonexistent.

"Okay, girl. Next party, be there." Maria paused for a moment and then asked, "How was your trip back to Atlanta? Did you see him?"

Toni sighed as she kicked off her shoes and finally dumped her bags onto the sofa. "I saw him. We screwed. I left."

"Toni!"

"What? We were both mature adults about it. We were there, we were horny, so we did it. There's nothing wrong with having sex with an ex, as long as both of you know that's all it is."

"So does he know?" Maria asked.

"Does he know what?"

"That that's all there is?"

She thought he did; but after a few drinks, Brian had

made it clear he wasn't over her. "It doesn't matter," she finally said, shrugging off the guilt. "It's over now."

"Code for: you're just not going to take his calls."

"Wow. Why are you taking this so personally? You're acting like Brian is your brother or something."

"You stay the hell away from my brothers."

"What?"

"C'mon. If you were a guy, you would be what *we* women would call a dog. You're a wham-bam-thank-you-ma'am kind of girl."

"That's not true. Brian and I had a little office fling a few years ago and it just didn't work out. End of story."

Maria laughed. "You have to have more than sex to have a relationship, Toni."

"When you're as busy as I am, it's hard to find time to have more than just sex. I work ninety hours a week in a law office that expects a hundred and the only vacation I get is our annual December weekend trip."

For the past twenty years Toni and her college friends Brooklyn, Maria, Ashley, and Noel would travel to New York for holiday shopping and Broadway plays. Like her best friend Brooklyn, Toni didn't think the girls got together enough, but as each of them had such busy lives, one weekend was better than nothing.

Toni and Brooklyn had once lived just miles apart in Atlanta, but once Brooklyn remarried and moved to Texas, Toni decided it was time for a change, as well, and high-tailed it to L.A. and now lived just miles from Maria.

Ashley still worked at the American Embassy in England. Noel resided in New York but was no longer "the only white girl in rap," as they once teased.

The only evicted member from their group was Macy Patterson and that was only because she had broken a golden girlfriend rule: sleeping with and then stealing Brooklyn's first husband.

Maria laughed and brought Toni's thoughts back to the present. "Hold on. Let me get my violin out."

"Not funny." Toni made her way to the kitchen and grabbed a soda. Maybe she shouldn't have slept with Brian. He was always the overly emotional type. She was only in Atlanta to help her practice with one of her old cases, but one night one thing led to another.

"Did you at least win the case?"

"Of course." Toni popped the cap off her soda and took a deep celebratory chug. "Toni Wright never loses a case."

"I got to hand it to you, Toni. You are good."

"In six months, I'll be a full partner at Kaplan, Grey & Kaplan. Mark my words."

Maria sighed as if indifferent to the idea.

"What?" Toni asked defensively.

"What what?"

"C'mon, what's with the long sigh?"

"Nothing," Maria lied unconvincingly.

"Spit it out." Toni left the kitchen and made a beeline to her bedroom and into the adjoining bath-

room. "If you have something to say just say it." She
plugged the tub and turned on the water.

"Well, it's just that everything is always business with you."

"A minute ago you said it was sex."

"All right. Business and sex. What about romance? When are you going to find a guy and just
settle down?"

"Oh, not that again," Toni moaned, and took another swig of Diet Pepsi before reaching for her bath
salts.

"Yes, that again. Don't you ever get lonely?"

"I don't have time to get lonely. Besides, marriage
isn't for everyone. If I see too much of someone I
just break out in hives."

"That's not true."

"It feels true." Another chug. "You want to know
the truth?" she asked.

"Please."

"I get claustrophobic in relationships," she admitted. "Seeing someone day after day, night after
night. I don't see how people do it."

"Oh, God. Are you sure you don't have a penis?"

Toni laughed and shut off her bathwater. "I'm
sure." However an unexpected image of Jonas Hinton floated across her mind. "Besides, love is a
woman's greatest downfall," she quoted her mother.

"I don't believe that. But if you're happy, then I'm
happy."

"And I am," she reaffirmed; but after she ended
the call, the apartment's silence bothered her.

It was too quiet.

Then just as quickly, she laughed the whole notion off. "Don't let all that relationship talk get to you, girl. You like your life just the way it is."

Chapter 3

"The best thing for a hangover is another drink," Q announced, handing Jonas a tall, stiff one.

Jonas moaned, waved off the glass and stumbled to his feet. How did he allow himself to get in this condition? He was doing so well.

"Whatever you do, don't tell me you were drinking over *her* again," Q said, keeping the vodka for himself and eyeing his oldest brother. When Jonas didn't respond, he had his answer. "See? This is what I've been trying to tell you and Sterling," he continued. "When it comes to women, keep your emotions out of it."

"Somehow I keep forgetting you're an expert." Jonas wavered on his feet but managed to make it to his adjoining bathroom and, more mercifully, the shower.

The icy water was more than enough to quell his nausea and clear his foggy head while he repeated the vow he'd made over a year ago. "Never again."

By the time Jonas stepped out of the shower, he'd nearly transformed into a human Popsicle. But at least he wasn't hungover.

"I don't know how the hell you do that," Q said, draining the last of his drink and standing up from the leather chaise inside his brother's bedroom.

Jonas didn't know how his brother always had a way of looking like he was ready for a *GQ* photo shoot. His hair and clothes were always picture-perfect and his eyes were always clear despite a hangover.

"Why are you here?"

"I need a favor."

"If it involves money, the answer is no."

"C'mon, I'm good for it."

"No, you're not. When Mom and Dad cut you off, they didn't mean for you to come crawling to me to support you. Get a job."

Q shuddered repulsively and held his fingers up like a crucifix.

"Not funny. Get a job." Jonas finished toweling off and pulled out a pair of silk boxers. Every week they had this same conversation about Q's financial situation and the result was also always the same: Q would avoid joining the work force by finding some gullible, wealthy woman to take care of him.

"Look, everyone will be a lot better off if they just

accept I'm not like you and Sterling. I have no business in Corporate America."

"Then do something else," Jonas responded without sympathy, and selected a suit from his closet. "Find something you're good at and do it."

Q fell silent.

"There has to be *something*," Jonas added, though he was hard-pressed to think of anything himself.

"Well, I am good with the ladies," his little brother bragged with a jiggle of his eyebrows. "I haven't had a dissatisfied customer yet."

Jonas finally stopped and looked at him.

"I'm talking about bedroom performance only," Q amended. "I'm no good with that sticking around stuff."

"Q, grow up. You're thirty-three years old, still trying to live off Mommy and Daddy's money."

"Spare me the speeches, Jonas. A simple yes or no to the loan will suffice."

"Then the answer is no."

"Big surprise." Q turned toward the door.

"You want a surprise, ask me a different question," Jonas said.

"What—and miss out on our precious brotherly chats? Not on your life. Same time tomorrow?"

Jonas laughed. Q would never change. Their parents, an eccentric ex-Broadway actress and a much older real-estate tycoon were fair as far as parents went, and they always encouraged their sons to work hard and pursue their dreams. It worked for Jonas and Sterling who were both wealthy men in their own right; however, Quentin only pursued having a good time.

His father's new strategy was to cut Q off. Jonas and Sterling agreed not to offer any financial support. Six months later, Q was still living the high life. All in all, he was one lucky son of a bitch.

Jonas, however, delved in an array of business adventures. Once upon a time, *Business Week* magazine had hailed him as the CEO with the Midas Touch. Lately? Not so much.

Since his disastrous wedding, he seemed to have lost his mojo. No matter what he did, he was unable to get it back.

He would, he vowed. He had to.

Jonas quickly finished getting dressed and as he grabbed his keys and wallet from his clothes from the day before, Toni's business card flittered to the floor. He stared at it and then slowly reached for it. Instantly a smile curved his mouth, just thinking about the attractive attorney with the come-hither eyes and seductive perfume.

Her casual attire just hinted at the curves that lay beneath and he had to admit, although grudgingly, he was curious.

Turning, he walked to the phone next to the bed and started dialing the number on the card. On the first ring, his conscience asked: *what the hell are you doing?* On the second ring, he realized he didn't know. By the third ring, he started to hang up when the call was transferred to voice mail and Toni's sexy, almost husky, voice greeted him.

He listened to her leave-a-message spiel, all the while smiling at his last image of her; but when he heard the beep, he hung up.

"Don't be stupid, Jonas. You're not ready."

"Do you think a man could be too handsome?" Toni asked Maria out of the blue while picking over her meal.

Maria's heavily Botox'd face already held a look of surprise. "What do you mean?"

Toni shrugged as a way to downplay her question, but in truth, she hadn't been able to get Jonas Hinton's pretty-boy looks out of her head. Those curly lashes and deep-pitted dimples, and he had an adorable mole on the line of his jaw that she'd noticed during their long talk.

"I don't know," she finally said. "There was this guy I met yesterday—"

"Yesterday? You mean, on the airplane?"

"Actually, the bar at the airport."

"Sheesh. You're picking up men at the airport now?"

"Yeah. Yeah. I know it's nowhere as respectable as the grocery store." The barb was a direct hit, since it was well known between the girlfriends that Maria would spend hours on hair and makeup before trolling the wine and beer aisles at her local Albertsons.

"Men have to eat."

Toni just shook her head.

"What?" Maria asked with her defenses high.

"Nothing. It's just that…"

Maria crossed her arms as a sign of annoyance, but her expression remained the same. "It's just what?"

"Well…do you ever think that maybe you try a little too hard?"

Her friend jerked back as though she'd been slapped.

"I mean, you're a beautiful woman and you have a lot to offer, but you have this habit of acting like you're the last item in a bargain bin."

"Excuse me, ladies," the waitress interrupted. "How is everything?"

Toni welcomed the interruption; she suspected Maria was just on the edge of ripping her a new one for brute honesty.

"The food was wonderful. Thank you." To her surprise, the waitress placed a new apple martini in front of her. "I didn't order another drink."

"This is from the gentleman at the bar," the waitress informed her with a smile and then placed a business card down in front of her.

She and Maria turned in their seats to see a handsome blond-haired and blue-eyed gentleman holding up his drink in salute.

Toni smiled and nodded her thanks. "Chase Tillman," she read the card.

Maria, however, folded her arms and stabbed her with an icy glare. "You just attract all shapes and sizes, don't you?"

"What is that supposed to mean?"

It was Maria's turn to be blasé. "Nothing. I mean,

everywhere we go, men are always buying you drinks or slipping you business cards. Meanwhile, I can have a friggin' neon sign on my head and no one gives me the time of day."

Toni sighed. How do you go about telling someone that men, animals that they are, could sense desperation off a woman? Men respond to confidence.

"I have to get back to the office," Toni said, taking a healthy sip from her new drink and then reaching for her purse. "Lunch is on me."

Maria pressed her lips into a hard line and also reached for her purse.

Toni wished she could say something more encouraging to her old college friend, but it wasn't like they hadn't had this conversation before. It's inhumane to keep beating a dead horse.

"Are you going to call him?" Maria asked when Toni slipped her admirer's card into her purse.

Toni flicked another look at the man at the bar but could feel nothing but disappointment that he wasn't her airport dreamboat. "I don't know. I might. After all, Atlanta was Atlanta and this is L.A."

"I never knew that you were into the interracial dating thing."

Toni laughed. "Honey, when it comes to men, I'm an equal opportunity kind of girl."

Jonas had long suspected that he wasn't the easiest person in the world to work for; but at least there was one woman in his camp that was more than up for the challenge: Michelle Gunn.

For the past ten years, Michelle made sure every-thing in Jonas's life—personal and business—ran smooth. Her job title was personal assistant, but Jonas had long thought of her as his right hand.

"You've been drinking," Michelle stated after a brief glance in his direction.

"Shh. Don't call my parents."

Michelle's normally friendly expression failed to crack a smile.

Convinced there was a judgmental glint in her eyes, Jonas experienced a wave of irritation. "I don't have a problem," he hissed under his breath.

Michelle just turned away. "Your schedule is sit-ting on your desk and Sterling is waiting in your office."

He was the boss, yet he was the one being dis-missed. Definitely another sign of the direction his life had taken.

"Morning, Sterling," Jonas greeted as he breezed into his office.

Sterling stood from the leather couch and glanced at his watch. "Actually, it's noon." His gaze followed Jonas to his chair. "You've been drinking?"

"What? Do I have a sign on my head?"

"Your eyes. They're bloodshot. Plus, yesterday would have been the anniversary of—"

"Yeah, yeah. I know. I'm over it."

Sterling lifted a dubious brow and slid his hands into his pants pockets. "Are you honestly going to tell me that you didn't spend the day remembering what could have been?"

The problem with trying to lie to not only your brother, but your best friend, is that it's a waste of time. After all, it had been Sterling who'd clued him in on his wedding day that he was about to marry a woman in love with someone else.

"I'm not going to tell you anything, Mr. Know-it-all." Jonas plopped into his chair. "What do you want?"

"I have a business proposition for you." Sterling waltzed over to Jonas's desk and planted his hands. "I'm talking about a business deal that's also going to help you reap a little revenge on Solomon Bassett."

"I'm listening."

Revenge is a dish best served cold....

Chapter 4

Six months later...

"It's not you. It's me," Toni told Chase over the phone. Her spring fling with the business manager had finally limped on its last legs and it was time for her to move on.

Toni was a Georgia Peach, no matter how hard she tried to meld into the L.A. scene. In the end, she turned down a partnership at her practice, and was now packing up her things to return to Atlanta.

"What? Was it something I did?" he asked, sounding shocked by this latest development.

Toni tried her best to reassure him that he'd done nothing wrong, but it didn't sound as though he believed her. In the end, he accepted the breakup, and asked her to call if she ever changed her mind.

Maria hated to see her go, but understood Toni had to do what was best for her.

When she landed at Hartsfield-Jackson Airport, an old memory stirred as she walked past the Crown Room and she was even tempted to poke her head into the bar to see if a familiar face with deep dimples could be found in the crowd.

She didn't.

She'd left the ball in Jonas's court and he'd never bothered to contact her.

C'est la vie.

There were definitely other fish in the sea and she was determined to catch as many as she could.

Instead of transferring back to the Atlanta branch of Kaplan, Grey & Kaplan, Toni decided that it was time to open her own law practice. Gutsy, but suddenly a necessity. Her friends had asked whether she was going through some type of midlife crisis. Maybe she was, maybe she wasn't. She just needed a change—a challenge. A few weeks later, the law office of Toni Wright was in business.

As luck would have it, her first client would bring back an old familiar name.

Solomon Bassett had to sit down.

"I see you're as shocked as I am." Marcel Taylor, president of T&B Entertainment, stood up from behind his desk and began pacing the long length of his office. "That man is out to destroy this company."

Solomon was too angry to speak, but his hands clenched and unclenched at his side.

"Fifty percent stake in *our* company. What the hell?" Marcel paced some more. "This is war. You know that, don't you?"

"I'll kill him," Solomon finally seethed. "He steps one foot in this building and, I swear, I'll kill him."

"Stand in line." Marcel's pace quickened. "How could Warner screw us like this? We should have had first dibs to purchase their share in T&B."

"They assured us they wouldn't sell their share. Our profits are solid. We have eight acts currently in the top twenty on *Billboard.* How could they do this to us?"

"We should have checked into this when Warner's financial troubles were first reported six months ago," Solomon groaned. "Fifty percent. That makes him an equal partner."

Marcel and Solomon fell silent as they continued to reel from the news of Jonas Hinton Enterprises purchasing Warner Music Group's stake in their company. What did it mean? What would their new partner do? Hell, did he even know anything about the music business?

"Mr. Taylor?" Kathleen, Marcel's latest secretary, buzzed him over the intercom.

"Not now, Kate!"

"Um. There's a Jonas Hinton here to see you."

"I said— What?"

Solomon bolted up from his seat.

"Mr. Hinton," she stated again, and then lowered her voice to whisper, "He insists that you want to see him."

Marcel glanced over at Solomon.

"He's a bold asshole, isn't he?"

"Send him in."

Solomon and Marcel drew a deep breath and attempted to collect themselves, but the moment Marcel's door opened, Solomon launched across the room with murder in his eyes.

"You vindictive son of a bitch!"

Jonas had just cleared the doorway before being tackled to the floor. Years of wrestling with his brothers also gave him an advantage in successfully hauling Solomon off of him.

"Get your boy before I hurt him," he barked.

Marcel hesitated, undoubtedly weighing whether he wanted to interrupt or jump into the match himself.

Solomon threw a one-two punch.

Jonas ducked one, but caught the second one dead in his mouth. He retaliated with his own punch and watched Solomon's head snap back with a resounding crack.

Marcel finally jumped into the fray and for a frightening moment, Jonas thought he was actually going to have to take on both men…and likely lose, but instead Marcel pulled his best friend and business partner off of him.

"You have a lot of nerve showing up here," Marcel growled.

Panting, Jonas touched his lip and then tamped down his anger at the taste and feel of blood. "Why wouldn't I show up here? As a partner, I have a vested interest in how things are being run." He wobbled as he pulled himself off the floor.

"I'm sorry but I have to do this." Marcel stepped forward and sent his own punch careening across Jonas's hard jaw.

With a grunt, Jonas collapsed back onto the floor and literally warred with whether to throw caution into the wind and just take on the angry partners in an all-out brawl or continue to get his butt kicked. He wanted to show a little maturity about this. But damn it, he wasn't a saint.

"Are you two finished?" he croaked.

The two men above him grumbled something, but at least they backed up and gave him a little more space. Jonas refrained from thanking them while lumbering back to his feet.

"Just tell us why you did it," Marcel snapped.

"Humph. I know why he did it," Solomon sneered. "He's a sore loser."

Jonas laughed, though it was probably a dangerous thing to do.

"Are you going to deny it?" Solomon challenged.

He could, but it would be lying. He was a sore loser. "Let's just say that I'm in the business of making money and you two are my new cash cows."

"You're insane," Solomon challenged.

"Perhaps." Jonas dabbed his bleeding lip and waltzed to an empty chair across the room. "I'm going to forget this…outburst because I understand you two are a bit emotional right now. If I were in your shoes I might be a little angry myself."

Marcel and Solomon just watched their new partner make himself at home.

"Yes, well," Jonas continued when neither man spoke, "I just wanted to stop by and assure you both that you don't have to worry about me getting in the way around here. Judging by your profitable annual reports, you two are obviously good at what you do."

"So you're more like a silent partner?" Marcel asked.

"Silent may be stretching it a tad. I might show up for the occasional staff meeting. You know, sort of poke in and out from time to time. I might have a suggestion here and there."

"In other words," Solomon spoke up, "you're going to be a regular pain in the ass."

"Ah." Jonas's smile broadened. "Now, that sounds like a more accurate description."

By the time Jonas left T&B Entertainment, he was practically on cloud nine seeing the absolute misery on his new partners' faces. When Sterling first brought this investment venture to him, he thought the opportunity was too good to be true, and then he thought it all sounded too good to pass up.

But perhaps he did take things a little too far in the end when he inquired about Ophelia and the baby. If Marcel had not been in the room, Solomon would have been looking at a sentence of life without parole.

Regardless, Jonas slipped into his waiting limo with a smile on his face. He arrived at his new office in the heart of downtown Atlanta in less than twenty minutes.

"You have a visitor," Michelle informed him the moment he entered the office. "What happened to your face?"

"Nothing to concern yourself with," he assured her.

As far as Jonas was concerned, she could have told him it was time for a prostate exam and it still wouldn't have ruined his mood. "Send in whomever it is," he told her, and continued into his office.

He wanted to celebrate. He actually wanted to dance, which was probably not a good idea since dancing was not his strong suit. But he gave it a try anyway. He swiveled his hips, pumped his fist into the air and even combined it with some strange kick-boxing moves. All in all, he was feeling good.

"Should I call a medic?"

Jonas jumped and turned around. However, the last person he expected to see was standing in his doorway. "Toni."

Chapter 5

A wide smile eased across Toni's full lips. "You remembered my name." She closed the door behind her and glided into the room. "May I ask what has you in such a good mood? And did you catch the name of that train that ran into your face?"

Astonished, Jonas absently touched his swollen lip but couldn't quite find his voice. She looked good.

Damn good.

Her legs in her short, black mini business suit went on for forever, while the rest of her body curved like nobody's business. He'd never guessed all this lay beneath her casual jeans and plain top the last time he'd seen her.

"I take it you're surprised to see me?"

"That's putting it mildly," he managed to say. "This office just opened."

"Yes, I know."

He frowned, not knowing how to take that answer. "Um. Look, I was meaning to call you," he began.

"No, you weren't," she said, smiling. "But it's kind of you to lie." Toni moved farther into the room, glancing around as if she was inspecting the place. "Nice."

"Thanks." He waited, wondering wildly why she was there; but when it was apparent that she wasn't giving the information freely, he decided to prompt her. "Just in the neighborhood?"

"No. I came to see you," she said with a teasing wink. "And I must say you're looking extremely well. At least you're not drowning your sorrows at a bar."

Jonas tensed.

Her gaze raked him openly. "You sure know how to fill out a suit, Mr. Hinton."

The tension left Jonas as a smile returned to his lips. "If I didn't know any better I'd say you were flirting with me."

Her eyes caressed him once again. "I like flirting with you—even though it doesn't seem to have much effect."

Judging by his quickening pulse and the room's rising temperature, she was definitely wrong about that.

"Or does it?" she asked.

"Are you trying to get inside of my head?"

Their gazes locked.

"I can think of something else I'd rather get into."
Her eyes dropped to below his waist.

Her boldness startled him and he turned away
before she could see how much her teasing was
actually getting to him. When he reached his desk,
he used it to literally hide his growing erection.

Toni's eyes twinkled like she knew exactly what
he was doing. With a widening smile, she followed
and approached the desk like a lioness stalking its
prey. "You're not afraid of me, are you?"

Jonas forced out a laugh from his tight chest, but it
only succeeded in widening his huntress's smile. "I'm
not afraid, but you have that look in your eyes again."

"What look?"

"That I-can-eat-anyone-alive-and-still-have-room-
for-dessert look."

She stopped at his desk and set down her briefcase.
"Relax. I'm not going to bite…unless you want me
to?"

An image of a naked Toni crawling on top of him
and nibbling at his bare flesh sent a delicious shiver
down his spine.

"Ooh. Is that a spark I see?" she asked.

Horror of all horrors, Jonas felt an embarrassing
heat rush up the column of his neck and then burst
into his face. He was blushing. The woman actually
made him blush.

Toni laughed and finally settled into a chair across
from his desk. "All right, dimples. I'll take it easy
on you. As much fun as this is, I didn't come here
for a lunchtime quickie or even for a reunion."

Still suffering from the room's rising heat, Jonas leaned back in his leather chair, fingered his collar and wished the blood pulsing in *both* heads would ease. "What did you come here for?"

"Business." She reached for her briefcase and pulled out some papers. "You're being sued."

Ophelia loved being married, but loved being a mother even more. As she strolled through the doors of T&B Entertainment, wearing a wide smile and bouncing baby Imani on her hip, Paula leaped up from behind the reception desk and led the charge to surround Ophelia and coo silly baby talk at the newborn.

"She's so adorable. How old is she now?"

"Seven months," Ophelia boasted proudly. "She looks more and more like her father every day."

Paula leaned back and studied Imani cramming her fist into her mouth. "She might have his nose and cheeks but she definitely has your eyes."

Ophelia flushed, but continued to beam at her bundle of joy while more women at the record label, which were most of the employees, tickled, pinched and kissed Imani.

"We've come to take my adorable husband to lunch, please tell me he's not in some stuffy meeting."

A few of the women gave cursory glances at each other that pricked Ophelia's curiosity. "Is something wrong?"

"Oh, no," Paula covered, but obviously no one ever told her she was a bad liar. "Um, he should be up in his office. I'll just buzz Chelsea and let her know you're on your way up."

"Mmm. Okay." Ophelia glanced to the other women; however, they all suddenly got very busy and had to rush off for one thing or another. None of this was a good sign and it instantly had Ophelia suspecting bad news.

And she was right.

"Jonas did what?" she thundered incredulously.

An angry Solomon paced the length of his office and Ophelia swore she saw steam billowing from his ears. "You should have warned me about how vindictive this man is. He can't have you so he's decided to go after my company!"

Hearing her father's angry tone, Imani scrunched her face and began to cry.

Ophelia immediately huddled her daughter close to comfort her.

Instantly contrite, Solomon stopped his angry prowl and went to his favorite girls. "Oh, my baby." He held out his arms and Imani reached for him. The moment she was in his arms, the crying stopped.

Ophelia rolled her eyes and pretended to be wounded. "She's going to be a spoiled daddy's girl."

"Yeah." Solomon grinned at his wife. "Just like her mother."

After giving him a playful pop on the shoulder, Ophelia returned back to the business at hand. "Did he say why he bought shares of the company?"

Tensing but maintaining his smile, Solomon continued to bounce his daughter in his arms. "It's pretty obvious why, don't you think?"

"Well, I just can't believe that he would be malicious about what happened... I mean, we both stopped the wedding because I..." She sighed. "Maybe I should go talk to him?"

"Over my dead body," Soloman roared.

Imani started crying again.

"Oh, Daddy's sorry." Solomon cooed, and kissed his baby's forehead. Again, the tears stopped instantly. "You," he said pointedly at his wife, "stay away from that jerk. Marcel and I will handle it. Hinton has another think coming if he thinks this is just going to be another company he collects and plays puppet master."

"He's actually a pretty good businessman," Ophelia said, and then realized her mistake.

"Are you defending him now?"

"Of course not." She tried to win him over with an innocent smile. "I'm just saying..."

"What?"

Noticing the hardening of her husband's jaw, Ophelia recognized a lost cause when she saw it. "Nothing. You're right. Jonas has definitely crossed the line on this."

Solomon didn't respond. He just studied her as if he'd never seen her before.

Ophelia continued to smile to get back in his good graces. "Anyway, Imani and I were hoping you could join us for lunch. Diana had to back out to take her grandmother to a doctor's appointment."

Solomon sighed with regret. "I wish I could but Marcel and I have a one-o'clock conference call with Dawson Smith at Warner."

"Oh. Well, okay. I guess it's just you and me, Imani." She reached for her daughter, but she turned away to stay in her father's arms.

"I'm sorry, honey, but we have to get to the bottom of this and see what our options are."

Ophelia clamped her mouth shut.

"Rain check?" he asked.

"Of course. Your credit is always good with me." She kissed him soundly on the lips. "I hope this doesn't mean you'll be working late," she whispered. "I have a little sumpthin' sumpthin' planned tonight."

"Oh?" Solomon's brows lifted. "Do I get a hint what this surprise entails?"

Ophelia slyly pecked his lower lip. "Well, it *might* involve cherries, whip cream and…" she nibbled on the side of his lips "…a blindfold."

A wide smile slid across Solomon's face as he covered one of Imani's ears. "We shouldn't talk of such things in front of the *b-a-b-y*."

"Mum's the word." She winked. "I'll see you at home." She finally extracted her daughter from her cocoon and had to soothe her instant tears. However, during her exit out of T&B Entertainment, her mind wandered back to Jonas.

"Hold on, honey," she told her daughter as she strapped her into the car seat. "We have one more stop before we head out to lunch."

Chapter 6

"What?" Jonas jumped to his feet, forgetting about his monster hard-on. "Who's suing me?"

Toni's gaze lowered to his impressive tented pants, and then climbed back up in time to see the blood drain from Jonas's face. "You like me. You really, really like me."

Jonas lowered himself back into his chair, shifting the power ball back into her court. "Who is suing me?"

"Actually the suit is against the owners of T&B Entertainment. Imagine my surprise when I saw your name listed on the suit as part owner." She cocked her head. "I guess you couldn't let sleeping dogs lie?"

Fascination shifted to irritation and Jonas's eyes narrowed. "It's strictly business."

She smiled and called him on the lie. "No, it's not."

"Then how about it's none of *your* business?" he asked instead.

"Ah, just like a man. You reel me in and then you shut me out." She tossed up her hands. "*C'est la vie.* But you're still being sued."

"And I'm still waiting to find out by whom."

"An ex-employee of T&B Entertainment, Nora Gibson. She filed a wrongful-termination suit."

Jonas rolled the name around his head. "I know her," he said, thinking. "I met her at Marcel and Diana's wedding. She sort of puts me in mind of a piranha."

"I'd prefer if you would refrain from calling my client names."

Rolling his eyes, Jonas reached for the papers Toni had flung on his desk. "What? She filed this suit in L.A.?"

"No."

He lifted a brow as he casually flipped through the pages. "Then how did she hire you?"

"Not that it's any of *your* business but I live in Atlanta now."

"Kaplan, Grey & Kaplan must be disappointed."

"But I'm ecstatic, and that's all that matters." She slowly crossed her legs.

Jonas watched her long limbs like a starved man before a Thanksgiving feast while a thousand questions raced through his mind. Were her legs as soft as they looked? What would they look like wrapped around his waist? His shoulders?

Toni's light laughter snapped him out of his daydream and for the second time, he blushed.

"One million to make the suit go away," she said.

It was Jonas's turn to laugh and he did so with a hearty gusto. "You've got to be kidding me."

"I don't kid about such things," she informed him with a leveled stare. "Believe me, you're getting off easy."

Jonas quirked his brow; but when the attractive attorney remained serious, his inner voice shouted for him to take the deal. "I'll need time to review the case."

"Certainly." Toni climbed back onto her feet and wasted no time heading toward the door. "It was great seeing you again."

"Same here." With his pants still tented in high salute, Jonas remained seated, but experienced a rush of disappointment to see her leave.

"You know," she tossed over her shoulder as she sashayed toward the door, "acts of revenge never pan out." She paused after opening the door. "I thought you were over her?"

Just like that, Jonas's irritation returned. "We went over this. It's none of your business."

Toni shrugged. "Good luck." She glided out of his office with a nod toward Jonas's assistant. However, on her way to the elevator bay, she grumbled about Hinton's hardheadedness. This Ophelia chick must have really been something to work a number on him like this. Actually, she didn't know whether to admire or be jealous of the woman.

The elevator doors slid open and an attractive woman, pushing a baby stroller, emerged.

"Excuse me." The woman stopped her. "Could you tell me which office is Jonas Hinton Enterprises?"

"Oh, yes." Toni smiled. "I just left there. If you turn down that hallway over there," she pointed, "it's the last office at the end of the hall."

"Thank you."

"Don't mention it." Toni turned back to the elevator, but the doors had slid closed and she had to punch the down button again. A minute later, the second elevator's door opened and she rushed to jump inside before the fast doors closed on her again. Unfortunately, she jumped right into the arms of a man, exiting.

"Whoa, there."

"Oh, I'm sorry." She laughed and then glanced up. She gasped at the man who could have easily passed as Jonas's twin, except for his thin, groomed goatee.

The elevator doors closed.

"No need to apologize," he said; his gaze traveled down the length of her frame. "It's not every day a beautiful woman leaps into my arms."

"I find that hard to believe." She flirted back.

"Going down?" he asked.

Toni's brows rose.

"I meant, are you going down to the lobby," he clarified with a nervous laugh.

"Oh, well. In that case, yes, I am."

He punched the L button and turned back toward her. "Sterling Hinton." He thrust out a hand. "And you are?"

Toni eyed the hand and the man before deciding to roll with it. "Toni Wright." She eased her hand into his just as the elevator jerked to a stop.

Toni dropped her briefcase and crashed back into Sterling. "What on earth?"

The lights flickered overhead.

"I think we have a situation," Sterling announced, and proceeded to jab the lobby button again. "We're stuck."

A loud groan filled the small compartment above them and Toni's heart leaped. "Please tell me that's not the cable cords."

To Sterling's credit he remained calm during the crisis and looked her in the eye. "Actually, I'm embarrassed to say that it may be my stomach. I haven't eaten today."

Toni laughed, her fear dissipated. "It's not wise to skip meals."

"No?" he asked with a lifted brow. "Then I should definitely rectify the problem. Care to join me?" A deep smile stretched across his face. "You can make sure I eat all my vegetables."

Her smile grew. "I think I can handle that." She glanced at her watch. "*If* we get out of here anytime soon."

On cue, the elevator jerked.

Gasping, Toni clutched Sterling's arm, but then

sighed in relief when the elevator began its slow descent to the lobby.

"Well, look at that," he joked. "This must be a sign."

She smiled and gave him another glance over. "Must be."

Ophelia stopped in the restroom to give Imani a quick diaper change. After washing up and checking herself in the mirror, she realized she was nervous. The last time she'd seen Jonas was at the altar of their wedding.

He had looked so crushed and heartbroken...but he let her go, even though she knew he didn't want to.

She checked her appearance again, frowned at the extra ten pounds that hung around her waist but then chided herself before she started obsessing over it.

"All right," she said to her reflection. "You can do this."

But she didn't move.

When Imani squeezed her stuffed Leap Frog and the alphabet jingle echoed off the bathroom tiles, Ophelia finally jarred out of her reverie and marched out of the bathroom. However, the moment her hand turned the office door, a nest of butterflies fluttered in her stomach.

Michelle sat at her desk, her fingers flying over her keyboard while she talked simultaneously into her headset. However, all movement ceased when she looked up at the office's new visitor.

Ophelia fluttered a nervous smile. The two women were more than acquainted. Ophelia was Jonas's employee before she was his runaway bride.

"Hello, Michelle," she greeted, forcing more cheerfulness than was necessary. Her first sign that things weren't going to go so well was when the woman didn't respond. Instead, she just glanced over her like Ophelia was some troublesome loiterer and she was debating whether to call the police. "Um, is Jonas in?"

"Tariq, let me call you back." Michelle punched a button and removed her headset. "Actually, you just missed him."

"Oh." Ophelia glanced down at the stroller, reeling from the woman's coldness. "Well, um, can you at least tell him that I stopped by?"

Michelle stared pointedly at her. "Sure thing."

An awkward silence lapsed between the women before Ophelia maneuvered the stroller around and headed back out of the door.

"Michelle, contact Marcel Taylor..."

Ophelia froze at the sound of Jonas's voice, and then slowly glanced over her shoulder. Not surprising, her ex-fiancé was as handsome as ever and his sudden presence dominated the room. She expected to experience a ripple of guilt when she saw him again, but what she got instead was a tidal wave.

Jonas's shocked gaze roamed over her as if he didn't trust his eyes.

"Jonas," she whispered, and then shot an accusatory glare at Michelle. "You *are* here."

Undaunted at being caught in a lie, Michelle returned her attention to her computer and gave a lousy performance of minding her own business.

"What are you doing here?" he asked, finding his voice.

Ophelia drew a deep breath and summoned a small batch of courage. "I came to ask you to back off."

Toni rewarded Sterling with a smile when he held out her chair for her at Houston's. Chivalry should not be overlooked in this day and age and so far Jonas's younger brother had it in spades.

"This must be my lucky day," he said, taking his seat. "A trip to one of my favorite cities and now lunch with a beautiful woman."

"Handsome *and* charismatic," she noted. "I must be experiencing a little luck myself." When he flashed a smile, she experienced a small jolt of disappointment that he didn't inherit his older brother's adorable dimples.

"Is something wrong?" he asked.

"Um, no." She made a half attempt to wave off his concerns. "I was just thinking...forgive me."

Sterling grimaced. "If your mind is wandering then that means that I should double up on the charm." He leaned toward her. "Has anyone ever told you that your eyes sparkle like diamonds?"

Cheesy but cute.

"And you're even more beautiful when you smile?"

Toni marveled over the differences between the two brothers. Whereas Jonas was guarded and even a bit moody, Sterling was open and available. However, try as she might, she couldn't get herself to stop comparing the two and preferring the eldest.

With Jonas she was boldly flirtatious, with Sterling she felt reserved and dared she say: stifled?

Sterling struck her more as a model Boy Scout—too good to be true.

After the waiter appeared and then reappeared with their drink order, Sterling continued to pile on the compliments, winning so many brownie points that Toni accepted a second date.

When one door closes another one opens, right?

"Maybe we should take this into my office?" Jonas offered, and then turned to Michelle. "Hold my calls."

Michelle's lips puckered like she'd been sucking on a lemon. "You're the boss."

Ophelia wheeled the stroller around, took another deep breath and marched into Jonas's office. With each step, the knots in her stomach tightened and her heart rate climbed to a dangerous level. Out of all the emotions swirling inside of her, so far she had managed to keep regret at a manageable distance.

However, if her husband ever found out that she was here…

Jonas closed the door behind them. "I have to say you're certainly looking good. Marriage agrees with you." His gaze swept down to the sleeping baby inside the stroller and a soft smile tugged his lips. "Or is it motherhood?" He glided past her and took his seat behind the desk. "Now, what's all this talk about me backing off?"

"Why did you buy Warner's interest in Solomon's company?"

"C'mon, Ophelia. You've always known that I'm a voracious businessman. I go where the opportunities and the money leads me. This time, it just so happened to lead me straight to T&B Entertainment."

"A convenient coincidence, don't you think?"

"Is there any other kind?"

Ophelia sucked in an impatient breath. "So we're going to just play games and act like you don't know what I'm talking about?"

Jonas sat back in his chair; his gaze roamed the length of her like a habit he couldn't break—or didn't want to break. "Letting you go was the most difficult thing I've ever had to do. I'll admit that." He braided his fingers. "I'm not accustomed to being embarrassed in front of six hundred friends and family."

"So this is all about us?"

"All? No." He smiled.

Ophelia stared, contemplating her next chess move. Logic wouldn't appeal to a man motivated by emotion. "What happened between us wasn't intentional. I did care for you. And—"

"Spare me." Jonas stood and eyed her cagily as he moved around his desk and leaned against one corner. "We've already been over this ground. I'm such a good man and one day I'll make some lucky woman a wonderful husband, blah, blah, blah. I remember the speech."

"Then what?" she snapped. "What do you *really* want from us?"

"I want…" He checked his anger and then smiled benignly. "I want just a little satisfaction. You and Solomon have been living happily-ever-after for the last eighteen months while my world has been turned upside down. I want you both to feel what I feel—just for a little while." He snapped his fingers as if suddenly remembering something else. "And to make a little money in the process."

"This is childish and I expected better from you."

Jonas's smile didn't falter as he pushed away from the desk and approached her.

Ophelia stood her ground and lifted her head defiantly when he stopped within inches of her and leaned close.

"A spoonful of sugar helps the medicine go down." He leaned forward.

"I know that asshole is here!"

Jonas's door flew open as Solomon breezed into the office and stopped short when his eyes landed on Jonas and Ophelia. "What the hell?"

Chapter 7

Out of all the duties that Michelle had to engage in over the years, one she hadn't expected was to act as referee and break up a fight. No sooner had Solomon barreled his way past her did the man launch at her employer's throat. Granted, Jonas had it coming since they'd walked in on him about to kiss his attacker's wife.

In order: Jonas writhed on the floor, Solomon was sprawled on top of him with a fierce choke hold, Michelle hopped on Solomon's back and hooked an arm around his neck in a less effective choke hold, Ophelia stood above everyone screaming for them to stop, while lastly, the baby woke and was wailing at the top of her lungs.

All in all, a circus no matter how you looked at it.

More voices thundered into the room, but no one paid them any attention. However, the next thing Michelle knew, she was plucked off Solomon's back and set aside. Another pair of arms broke Solomon's firm grip on Jonas's neck.

"Has everyone gone crazy?" Quentin thundered, helping his brother up from the floor.

"Sol, man, what's gotten into you?" Marcel asked, struggling to keep a hold on his best friend.

"I came up here and found these two…" His hard glare swung to Ophelia, but he never finished his sentence.

"It wasn't what it looked like," Ophelia defended, comforting the child.

"Really? Because it looked like he was about to kiss you!"

"Then it was what it looked like," Jonas said with a mocking smile and an indifferent laugh.

"I wasn't going to let you kiss me!"

"We'll never know. Now, will we?"

Solomon launched at him again, but Marcel tightened his grip and threw his whole body into keeping them apart. "Calm down, man. Calm down. We came here to make peace, remember?"

Finally Solomon stopped struggling and tossed his hands up in surrender. However, his accusing stare found Ophelia again. "And why did you come here? I remember specifically telling you not to."

His wife's chin came up in clear defiance, and

though she held her tongue, her eyes flashed with the promise that their argument would continue at another time.

"Maybe you all should leave," Q suggested. "Come back when everyone has cooled off."

"I think that's probably best," Marcel readily agreed; his own anger stabbing both Solomon and Ophelia. "I'll have Chelsea call and arrange a meeting."

Minutes later, Marcel successfully ushered his friends out of the office and left the Hinton brothers and Michelle alone to stare at one another.

"Man, I can't leave you alone for a moment," Q burst out with a hearty laugh.

Jonas rubbed at his neck, a red welt visible against his light complexion, and his busted lip bleeding again. "If you'd waited another minute, you'd be joking with a corpse right about now."

"That's usually the penalty for kissing a man's wife," Michelle chirped, and turned toward the door. "I'm taking the afternoon off. I need to rest my nerves."

Jonas knew better than to argue. "See you tomorrow?"

"We'll see."

Quentin did a lousy job muffling his amusement. "I take it your new partners aren't happy with your new business venture?"

"You can say that." Jonas returned Q's cocky smile. "Pity. I was hoping that we could all be fast friends."

Q turned toward one of the empty chairs and eased into it. "So you're kissing married women now?" His eyes twinkled as he laughed. "I don't think I've ever been more proud of you, bro."

"You have no idea how much that disturbs me." Still rubbing his neck, Jonas returned to his desk and reviewed what had just happened. He hadn't intended to kiss Ophelia. It was just that the urge came out of nowhere.

What did it mean?

Was he still not over her?

He shook his head. Maybe it was curiosity instead of attraction. When she stood before him, his body hadn't reacted the same way as it did when Toni was in his office.

With Toni, he hadn't so much as touched the woman and he'd been aroused to the point he wanted to knock everything off his desk and wrap those gorgeous legs of hers around his waist. Suddenly the room's temperature skyrocketed during his fantasy.

"Well?" Q prompted.

Jonas blinked out of his reverie. "Well, what?"

"Well, was it worth it?" Q laughed.

It was and it wasn't. It had been eighteen months and he could finally say that he was no longer in love with Ophelia. "Yes," he said, nodding.

Quentin's smile spread wider. "You old dog. I knew you had it in you."

Jonas just laughed. "Where's Sterling? I thought we all were going out to lunch?"

"He should have already been here. He left before I did." Q glanced at his watch. "We don't have to wait for him, do we? I'm starving."

"No. We can just call him on his cell phone on the way to the restaurant. He can just meet us over there." Jonas stood. "It's not like Sterling to be late. A woman must have caught his eye."

"Please." Q laughed. "Sterling is so straightlaced he wouldn't know what to do with a beautiful woman if one leaped into his arms."

Jonas did his best to clean up before he and Q headed out to lunch, but there was only so much one could do with a busted lip, a swollen neck and rumpled suit.

Quentin found the whole thing funny and emphasized how much he wished he could have been a fly on the wall.

"C'mon, man. It isn't like I've seen anyone kick your ass before," he goaded as they walked through the doors of Houston's. "Sterling came close that one time, remember? It was right after you stole his girlfriend and took her to the prom."

Affronted, Jonas's chest puffed out. "For the last time, I didn't steal Tracy Mathis from him. He never even told the girl he liked her. She was free game."

"Uh-huh. You ever think that Solomon stealing your girl from right under your nose was the universe's way of giving back what you put out?"

"Since when did you start believing in karma?"

Q shrugged. "This one chick I was seeing back in, um...April...or was it February? Anyway, she was real cool. Really into this spiritual stuff."

Jonas sighed. "What was her name?"

His baby brother's face drew a blank, just as he knew it would. "If this karma stuff is true then I don't want to be anywhere around you when you start getting your comeuppance."

"What? I spread love and happiness to beautiful lonely women. By my estimates I should be the next Powerball lottery winner."

Jonas opened his mouth for a rebuttal, but then thought better of it.

The hostess finally arrived at her podium. "How many are in your party?"

"Three. We're expecting one more," Jonas told her.

She nodded and reached for menus and silverware. "Follow me."

The brothers fell in line behind her and navigated through a maze of tables. Suddenly Q's hand clamped onto Jonas's shoulder. "Oh, there's Sterling."

Jonas stopped and followed Q's gaze.

"Looks like you were right. He did find a woman. A damn fine one at that."

Jonas had stopped breathing at the sight of Sterling and Toni hunched, laughing and ogling like a pair of lovebirds.

"Would you like to join them over there?" the hostess asked when she realized that they had stopped following her.

"No," Q said. "I think we should leave them alone. I haven't seen Sterling glow like that since Tracy Mathis." He started to walk away.

However, Jonas marched toward the couple.

"I stand corrected," Q said. "It looks like we will be joining them."

Damn right we are.

Enraptured by Toni's L.A. stories, Sterling didn't see or hear his brothers' approach; but when Jonas cleared his throat, he jumped as though he'd been caught with his hands in the cookie jar.

"Jonas. Quentin. What are you two doing here?" He frowned and did a double take on his older brother. "What happened to your face?"

"He got his ass kicked for kissing another man's wife." Q laughed.

Toni's brow shot up at the information.

"We were also all supposed to meet for lunch to celebrate Jonas's new business venture, remember?" Q asked.

While Quentin and Sterling chatted, Jonas's gaze zeroed in on Toni.

She returned his stare with a benign smile. "So we meet again."

Sterling and Q stopped talking.

"A constant but pleasurable occurrence," Jonas replied in his velvet baritone.

"You two know each other?" Sterling asked; his gaze ping-ponged between the two.

Toni curled toward Sterling, her smile turning syrupy. "We've met."

Suspicion crept into Sterling's handsome features.

"And the plot thickens," Quentin joked.

"Will you be joining this party?" the confused hostess asked.

"No/yes," Sterling and Jonas said in unison.

Q tried to suppress a grin while Toni's smile slid as wide as Texas.

The hostess remained standing with the menus suspended halfway toward the table.

Jonas pulled out a chair and sat down, all the while avoiding making eye contact with Sterling. "So how do you two know each other?" he asked. "I'd think that would be something that you would have mentioned."

Quentin hurried to take a seat so he could watch the drama unfold.

"We, uh, just met," Sterling grudgingly admitted, and then turned to Toni. "But, um, you didn't tell me you knew Jonas, either."

Toni shrugged their light interrogation off. "You didn't ask and I don't see why it's relevant. We have a business relationship. That's all."

Sterling visibly relaxed while Jonas clenched his jaw in irritation at the truth.

"Oh." Sterling perked. "For a minute there…"

"What?" Jonas challenged, finally finding his brother's gaze. "You thought it was something personal? Would you've backed off if there was?"

Caught off guard, Sterling searched his brother's face to judge whether he was being serious.

"There's no need to ask hypothetical questions," Toni said, rescuing Sterling. "The point is, there *isn't* anything between us." Her hand slid across the table and all three men's gazes tracked it until it covered Sterling's. "As far as Sterling and I, I'm open to the possibilities."

Sterling straightened in his chair as he sandwiched Toni's hand. "That makes two of us."

Jonas's gut clenched. *Over my dead body.*

Chapter 8

At the end of the day, Toni returned home exhausted and excited at the same time. One thing for sure, it was going to be a lot harder starting her own business than she initially thought. By harder, she meant more expensive. Licenses, office space, furniture and employees were draining her bank account so fast it made her head spin. Which was why when Nora Gibson walked through her office doors last week, she nearly wept with joy.

When she left home this morning, she never dreamed she would flirt with Jonas and then wrap his younger brother around her finger. Though it was a boost to her ego, there was no doubt she was in a tricky situation.

"It really is a small world," Toni told Maria over the phone after relating her day.

"That or it could be fate," Maria suggested.

"Fate?" Toni laughed. "Only hopeless romantics believe in such things. "I, on the other hand, believe in luck and opportunity. And I'm going to take this opportunity to get to know *Sterling* Hinton better."

"I can already tell you he's *not* the one for you," Maria said nonchalantly. "Pulling out your chair, ordering for you and showering you with compliments? He's too much of a Boy Scout."

"Does that mean I'll get a merit badge if I get him in the sack?"

"Hardly." Maria laughed. "It means you'll find him dull. Give you a brooding bad boy, however, and your panties practically melt off your body. You're weird like that. But if you want to send this Jonas Hinton out to California, then I'll gladly show *papí* a thing or two."

"It's bad form to beg for people's leftovers," Toni joked, but reflected over Maria's words. The problem with having lifelong friends is they had the tendency to know you better than you know yourself. What Maria so eloquently pointed out was one hundred percent true. Nothing turned Toni on more than a bad boy.

A challenge.

Looking back on that day in the airport, it had been Jonas's sullen and brooding mood that had caught her eye. Even today, though he struggled with restraint, Toni was certain there was a bad boy dying to get out.

The question was how to help him do just that.

"Are you there—or did you just call me to hold the phone?" Maria said, annoyed.

Toni blinked and retreated from her wandering thoughts. "Yeah, I'm still here. I just have a lot on my mind."

"Uh-huh. I was telling you I was thinking about getting my implants removed."

Toni rolled her eyes. "Didn't you just increase their size last year?"

"Yeah, but I'm starting to have some pain and swelling—not to mention half the time my back feels like it's going to snap in half."

Toni suppressed the urge to say "I told you so" and instead said, "You should definitely get it checked out. Are you just thinking about going down a size or…"

"I'm going to get rid of them altogether. See how I like being au naturel for a little while."

"Good for you," Toni praised, but in Maria's next breath, she was talking about the latest and great liposuction technique available, and Toni's mind wandered again. She continued to lend Maria half an ear while she ran bathwater and removed her makeup.

When the call finally ended, Toni soaked in a tub with lavender-scented bubbles while her mind replayed the scene in Jonas's office. However, her imagination altered things a bit and Jonas, instead of suppressing his attraction, had knocked everything from his desk, ripped off her clothes and screwed her brains out.

She had no doubts he knew his way around a

woman's body. Probably even knew a few tricks she'd never tried before, but ones she would be more than anxious to try.

Then her thoughts shifted to the restaurant. For as long as she lived there was no way she would ever forget the jealousy teeming in Jonas's eyes. Had Sterling been any other man, it was a safe bet that Jonas would have thrown a punch.

Hadn't the youngest brother said that Jonas had gotten his fat lip from kissing a married woman?

Her fantasy bubble popped. She was willing to stake her life that the married woman was Ophelia Bassett.

Aware of her bath's cooling water and vanishing bubbles, Toni quickly washed up and climbed out of the tub. When she finally curled into bed, she'd convinced herself she'd imagined Jonas's jealousy.

The phone rang and Toni rolled over to answer it. "Hello."

"I hope it's not too late to call."

Toni's heart raced. "Jonas?"

There was a pause and then, "No. It's Sterling."

Solomon took the couch. It had been hours but he could still clearly see his wife standing before Jonas with her chin lifted to receive a kiss. He would have never believed her capable of such a betrayal; but there she was, tearing out his heart.

"Sol, please come to bed," Ophelia said from the living room's doorway. She stood, arms crossed, in a sheer thigh-length nightgown and matching high-heeled slippers. "This is childish."

"Don't," he warned. "I didn't do anything wrong."

"Neither did I," she insisted. "I had no intentions of kissing him."

He jerked up to glare at her. "*He* had every intention of kissing you and I saw no resistance on your part."

"Sol—"

"You were going to kiss him in front of *my* child."

"She's *our* child," she snapped, and then quickly cooled off her temper. "Baby, I'm sorry. *But* nothing happened."

"Because *I* walked in." He shrugged. "Is that supposed to make me feel better? Nothing happened because I walked in?"

Her gaze fell from his to find a random spot on the floor.

Solomon whispered, "Do you still love him?"

Her gaze shot back up and her heart melted at the sight of his pain. "No, baby." She crossed the room to kneel before the couch. "Not in the way that you think."

He stiffened. "But you still have feelings for him?"

Ophelia took hold of her husband's hands. "I will always *care* for Jonas, but I'm not in love with him. I'm in love with you and no one else. Surely you can look into my eyes and see that I'm telling you the truth?"

Solomon did look into her eyes; seconds later a crooked smile jagged across his lips and he gathered her into his arms. "Oh, baby. I'm so sorry." He squeezed her tight. "I just feel that old jealousy curl in my gut whenever he's around."

"Shh. It's all right." She peppered kisses across his face. "Just know this—no man can ever take your place in my heart. I am your woman. Forever and always."

Solomon crushed her lips against his with an animal-like groan. He had loved this woman since June of '82 when they were thrown together in Ophelia's cousin's closet during the game Ten Minutes in Heaven. In that darkened closet, he had kissed a scrawny girl with a mouth full of wire and who smelled wonderfully of strawberry Bubble Yum. It was a kiss that had changed his life and enslaved his heart forever.

"C'mon, baby. Let's go to bed," Ophelia said.

"You got it." Solomon climbed to his feet and swept his wife into his arms and carried her off to the bedroom.

Jonas lost count of how many drinks he'd tossed back. All his thoughts and emotions were a complete jumble so he gave up trying to decipher them. It'd been quite a day, after all. He'd gotten his butt kicked—*twice,* nearly kissed his ex-fiancée and discovered his own brother dating his...what?

Technically Toni Wright was little more than an acquaintance. They'd shared drinks in a bar over six months ago. He had no claim on her.

Then why did it feel like Sterling had crept into his private safe and stolen his most prized possession?

"Women," he mumbled, pouring the last of the Jack Daniels.

Before Ophelia, Jonas had a slew of bad luck when it came to women. For the longest time, he seemed to only attract gold diggers or pampered trust-fund princesses. Both sets of women were void of any real emotion.

Ophelia was the first woman who didn't give a damn about his money and he was getting the same impression about Toni Wright. Yet, how could she flirt openly with him one moment and then curl in some dark corner with his brother the next?

Jonas drained the rest of his drink and then strolled across his penthouse to his opened window to stare out at the vast glowing lights along Atlanta's beautiful skyline. How sad it was to have everything that money could buy and still be the loneliest man on earth.

"I've become a walking, talking cliché," he grumbled, disgusted.

Exasperated, Jonas turned away from the window in a huff and nearly stumbled in the process.

"Whoa there," Q said, walking through the door with a girl hooked on one arm. "Are you having a private party in here?"

"Something like that," Jonas mumbled, and found himself envious of how his youngest brother moved from woman to woman with his heart still intact.

"Let me show you to my room," Q whispered to his playmate, and disappeared for a moment. When he returned, he approached Jonas with concern. "You all right, bro?"

"Never better."

Q nodded and slid his hands into his pockets. "You know, I was thinking. Maybe you should lay off the alcohol. Looks like you've been hitting it pretty hard."

Jonas bubbled with laughter. "What? You're trying to say I have a problem?"

"Do you?"

"Of course not," Jonas snapped, indignant. "I can quit anytime I feel like it." At the bar, he reached for another bottle.

"So why don't you try to quit now?"

"For the same reason you won't get a job—I don't want to."

Q cocked his head and continued to study him. "Then answer me this. What brought all this on tonight?"

Jonas didn't answer.

His brother crossed his arms. "This wouldn't have anything to do with Ophelia...or Sterling's new love interest, would it?"

Caught in the act

Chapter 9

"Alyssa," Beatrice, the waitstaff supervisor, called out at her and consequently gave away her position behind the Hintons.

Jonas peeked around the tree and grinned broadly down at her. "How long have you been there?"

Alyssa's face heated with embarrassment. "Not long," she lied.

Beatrice marched up to her like a wild twister in the middle of an Oklahoma tornado season. "I have the staff setting up the buffet tables, do you mind helping me take the tea trays up to the bride's suite?"

Alyssa perked up. "Sure!" It was her first chance to get a good look at Jonas's future wife.

The family, as well as the staff, was surprised and

curious about the woman who'd mended Jonas's heart and made him forget all about his ex-fiancée.

Alyssa and Beatrice loaded two serving carts and trekked to the east wing of the sprawling estate. As they approached the bride's suite, music and laughter spilled out into the hallway.

That magical buzz of excitement once again surrounded Alyssa and she couldn't wait to enter the room. The moment she did, it was like walking into Barbie's dream house. Beautiful women clustered together in different parts of the room. Some were getting their hair done, some their makeup, and in the center stood the bride in a gorgeous, shoulderless white dress.

The woman was practically glowing—and everyone knew why.

Alyssa sucked in a breath, convinced she'd never seen anything so beautiful in all her life. A real-life fairy-tale princess.

"Oh. The tea is here," one pretty woman exclaimed, and rushed over to the carts.

"Tea?" A Spanish beauty quipped. "Please tell me there's something a little stronger than that on the cart."

"You're in luck," Beatrice said; reaching underneath the cart to the hidden second tray, she pulled out a bottle of champagne, chilling in a bucket of ice.

"Whoo. That's what I'm talking about!" The Spanish beauty took hold of the champagne. "Now, let's get this party started."

"Maria, you just make sure that you save some for the others," the bride warned.

"Don't be mad just because you can't have any. What? Are those butterflies finally kicking in, Toni? It's not too late to plan an escape route."

Alyssa's heart clutched. The idea of another bride ditching Jonas at the altar scared her.

"I'm not going anywhere," Toni said, holding still for last-minute alterations. "It took me forty-three years to find a man I wouldn't mind waking up to for the rest of my life."

"Who knew he was younger than you?"

"He's not that much younger...just seven years."

"Humph! Seven years means that he was in eighth grade when you were graduating from high school," Maria said.

"And in elementary when you lost your virginity in the back of Jaron Miller's Hoopty," another woman added.

Alyssa quickly thought about the twenty-year difference between her and Quentin.

"Ashley, there's a young lady in the room," Toni reprimanded, and then smiled politely at Alyssa.

"Sorry," Ashley quipped.

"Aren't you a pretty little thing?" Toni inquired.

Alyssa looked around to see if she was talking to someone else.

"I'm talking to you," the bride reassured. "How old are you?"

"Th-thirteen."

"Ah, I remember thirteen," she said dreamily. "I received my first kiss at thirteen. Have you had your first kiss yet?"

Alyssa shook her head, but couldn't stop imagining a fantasy kiss with Quentin. He would pull her into his arms and…

"Aaah…so there *is* a boy you *want* to kiss," Toni said, reading her like an open book.

Alyssa dropped her gaze as her face heated.

All the women in the room noticed her reaction and chorused a long, "Aww."

"Well, we should be getting back to the kitchens, Alyssa," Beatrice said.

"Alyssa. What a pretty name," the bride cooed. "Oh, can't she stay and help us around here?" Toni asked.

Beatrice hesitated.

"I'm sure my dad won't mind," Alyssa said before Beatrice could make up an excuse.

"Then that settles it. You can stay and hang out with us."

Beatrice's lips pressed into a hard, firm line and her eyes flashed a warning to Alyssa to be on her best behavior before she backed out of the room.

"Alyssa, do you mind pouring my friends some tea?"

She shook her head and quickly went to work.

"So finish telling us how you snagged a ring from this young pup," another friend of the bride's asked. "I want details."

Alyssa's ears perked up. She was eager to hear more about Jonas and Toni's love story. Who knows, maybe she would learn a few pointers.

"All right. Well, like I said, I first started dating his brother…."

Chapter 10

Dating Sterling was hazardous to Toni's health.

On top of being the last Boy Scout, the man was a complete health nut. Biking, hiking and climbing rocks—Sterling was a gladiator out of time. One thing for sure: this was not how Toni liked to work out.

An aerobics class—sure.

A walk on the treadmill—fine.

Hot sex—count her in.

But working out like she's training for a triathlon—oh, hell no.

"Oh, that doesn't look too good," Sterling said, inspecting the bleeding scraped skin on her inner thigh. "Maybe mountain biking isn't your thing."

"What gave it away—my inability to stop or my being pitched head forward over the rails?"

Sterling chuckled but then apologized when she winced and then sucked in a pained gasp. "Hold still while I go get something to help clean and patch you up."

Toni nodded and admired his firm butt as he strolled out of the den. Was Jonas's butt that firm? She would definitely have to check it out the next time she saw him. Sighing, Toni's gaze floated around the Hinton brothers' luxurious penthouse. According to Sterling, the brothers shared a few properties in different cities for various businesses. Well, *except* Quentin who was apparently allergic to working—and crashed wherever he wanted.

Toni found the whole brotherly bond sort of cute—and problematic. She couldn't stop herself from constantly comparing one brother against the other and kept favoring the one she wasn't dating.

"Okay, here we go." Sterling returned with a bottle of alcohol, peroxide and a first-aid kit.

Toni tensed in anticipation of the alcohol burning her flesh wound. "You know, on second thought, I think it's fine."

"Come on. Don't wimp out on me," he coaxed with a wink. Had a woman ever been able to tell this man "no"?

Jonas breezed into the penthouse in a rush to pick up his golf clubs. There was no better way to spend his Saturday than on the green at his favorite country club. Truth be told, there was no better place to hear of business opportunities or stock tips.

"Oh, I don't know, Sterling." Toni's voice floated from the den just as Jonas marched by.

"C'mon. Open your legs for me."

Jonas stopped in his tracks and against his better judgment, he stole a peek into the room. From his angle he could only see the back of Toni's head.

"But right here?" She looked around.

Jonas jumped away from the den's entryway and pressed his body against the side wall to avoid detection.

"But can you even see what you're doing?" She laughed.

"Yes, yes. Now, stop stalling and spread your legs."

Jonas's eyes bulged and his hands clenched into tight fists.

"C'mon, just a little wider. That's my girl."

Toni sucked in a gulp of air through her teeth. "Sterling…"

"Relax. It's just going to hurt for a second and then you're going to adjust just fine."

Jonas felt nauseous. Were they actually about to get it on in the den—in the middle of the day? That sounded so unlike his conventional brother. But hell, a woman like Toni could talk a man into just about anything.

The front door opened and Jonas looked up to see Q strolling through the door.

"Hey, man. What's up? We going or not?" Jonas bolted toward the door, pressing a finger against his lip.

"What? What's going on?"

"Um, nothing. Let's go." He ushered Quentin back out the door.

"Wait. What about your clubs?"

"I'll borrow yours."

Quentin jerked back with an incredulous stare. "I don't have clubs. I use yours." He tried to push his way back into the penthouse. "What's going on? What are you trying to hide from me?"

"Nothing," Jonas lied. "Let's go. I'll buy a new set at the clubhouse." With one final shove, Q sailed out of the door while Jonas marched behind him, pissed.

Toni was sore all over.

The morning after her biking accident, she woke up a little stiff; but by Monday, muscles she had long forgot about ached to the point that she could barely move.

She had to end this relationship before it killed her.

"Toni Wright to see Jonas Hinton," she informed Michelle, who once again seemed like a one-woman show as she typed, talked and strolled through her day planner.

"I don't have you on the calendar," she said dully, and then continued ordering what sounded like office supplies.

"I know, but I'm sure Mr. Hinton would like to see me."

Michelle ignored her.

"Ma'am?"

"Hold, please." She punched a button on the console and lifted her narrowing gaze to Toni. "Ms. Wright, let's clear up some confusion. I know the name of this company is Hinton Enterprises, but make no mistake that this is *my* office. I run things here and I run a tight ship. And as part of that tight ship, I've implemented certain rules and procedures."

Toni retreated as the woman's voice rose sharply.

"I like rules and procedures, Ms. Wright. It has a way of making my life easier and therefore makes me happy. And if I'm happy, then you can rest assured my boss is happy, as well." She drew a deep breath. "Now. What have we learned?"

Toni was actually afraid to speak, but when it was clear that Ms. Gunn was growing impatient for her answer, she spoke timidly. "That you like rules and procedures."

"And?"

"And…if I want to see Mr. Hinton, I need to call and make an appointment."

Unbelievably a smile curled onto the assistant's face, transforming her into a very attractive woman. "Now. Would you like to make an appointment?"

"Sure."

Michelle faced her computer again and tapped a few keys. "You're in luck. He has an eleven-thirty available. Shall I add you in?"

"If it's not too much trouble."

"Don't be silly. That's why I'm here—to help."

* * *

As Jonas marched through the doors of T&B Entertainment with his no-nonsense lawyer, Patsy Nelson, at his side, he promised himself that he would be on his best behavior. In business, lawsuits were commonplace, but that didn't mean that Jonas was in the habit of losing.

On the contrary.

He prided himself for having the best legal team money could buy—which is where Ms. Nelson came in. Though he and the buxom attorney had a brief personal history, one dating back to before his meeting Ophelia, they had since kept everything strictly professional.

There were a few signs from Patsy that hinted she was open to picking things up where they'd left off. He'd even been tempted once or twice since his failed engagement to take her up on her offer, but so far, he'd refrained.

Now, whenever he looked at her, he couldn't stop himself from comparing her to another attractive attorney—one that had a pair of legs out of this world—and was currently dating his brother.

Not that he cared.

Meanwhile, he had a lawsuit to win. And the only way he could get down to the bottom of Ms. Gibson's lawsuit was to talk to her former employers. Marcel and Solomon.

"She's suing us?" Marcel and Solomon thundered at their attorney, Brian Olson, and then shot glances at Jonas and his attorney.

"For what?" Solomon added, though he had a sinking suspicion.

"Sexual harassment," Patsy filled in. "She's claiming that T&B Entertainment nurtures a hostile environment for women and that she felt objectified on a daily basis."

"What?" Marcel continued, outraged. "Who is she accusing of objectifying her?"

Olson glanced down and squinted through his reading glasses. "A William Bassett." He looked up at Solomon. "Any relation?"

Solomon groaned and slid deep into his chair.

"What?" Jonas asked suspiciously.

"He's my uncle."

Marcel just groaned.

Patsy straightened in her chair. "Are you telling me that her claims may be valid?"

"Hell, no," Solomon thundered. "Uncle Willy doesn't even *work* here."

"Not to mention Nora and Willy were in a relationship a couple of years ago. She's suing us because it didn't work out? Hell, I thought all that was settled when she gave him a black eye here in the office. You remember that, don't you, Sol?"

"How can I ever forget it?"

Olson picked up his pen and started scribbling. "Oh, this is good stuff. So you're saying this Willy character never harassed her here at the office?"

Marcel and Solomon looked at each other.

Jonas caught the shared look. "What?"

"Well, we didn't say that—exactly," Marcel corrected, and then looked to his partner for help.

"My, um, uncle is sort of a…colorful character when it comes to women."

Olson stopped writing. "How so?"

"Well." Solomon loosened his tie. "He's sort of an, um…"

"Yes?" Patsy probed.

"He loves women," Solomon finally settled on saying. "All women."

"However, the crazier, the better," Marcel tossed in for good measure.

"Uh-huh." Olson set down his pen and leaned back.

Solomon continued to struggle. "He may have, from time to time, made a sexual reference to some of the employees. But he never means anything by it."

"Unless they're willing to take him up on it," Marcel commented from the sidelines.

Solomon jerked his chair toward his friend. "You're supposed to be helping."

"Sorry."

Olson tossed up his hands. "Look, gentlemen. Maybe you should consider settling out of court. A jury could easily sympathize with the plaintiff on this. Employee or not, William Bassett is a relative of one of the owners and it could be construed that he's, in fact, an extension of yourself. If you allowed his… colorful behavior in the office unchecked, then…"

"You're supposed to be helping, too," Solomon reminded the lawyer.

"I'm not in the habit of settling," Jonas said, shifting in his chair.

"I just call it like I see it." Olson shrugged.

"I hate to admit it," Patsy chimed in. "It's no different than employees seeing your wives or significant others as someone with power within the office hierarchy. Ms. Gibson could come off as a sympathetic character."

"Words I never thought would be used in the same sentence," Marcel said.

"Ms. Gibson is asking for one million. I can try to talk her down to half. But that's a *big* if. She has a good lawyer."

"You know him?"

"Her," Jonas and Olson corrected. Everyone's gaze shifted to Jonas. "Ms. Wright and I met briefly," he answered.

The army of gazes then flew to Olson.

"Toni Wright," Olson agreed, nodding. "She's very good. She used to work at our firm…and we used to date."

Jonas's head snapped up. Damn, the woman got around.

Chapter 11

"Is something wrong, Jonas?" Patsy asked once they returned to the limousine. "You look as though you could chew nails."

Pulling his gaze from the side window, Jonas attempted to smile, but only one side of his mouth curled. "Everything is fine."

The look she gave said she didn't buy his answer. She shifted from the seat across from him to slide next to him. When she crossed her legs, she made sure that they rested on his. "What you need is to relax." Her fingers walked up the center of his chest and then loosened his tie. "You know my place isn't too far from here."

Jonas stared into her chocolate gaze, seeing nothing

but the promise of pleasure. But again, he found himself comparing Patsy's ethereal beauty to Toni's sultry beauty and grew frustrated in the process.

"That's not necessary, Patsy. I have a full day of work ahead of me. I need to get back to the office."

Instead of backing off, Patsy leaned close and nibbled on his ear. "We can always do it right here. You used to like that." The hand on his tie dropped suddenly to grab at his crotch.

Jonas launched out of his seat and landed on the opposite side of the limo. "Uh, I think I'm going to take a rain check. I really got…a lot on my mind."

Patsy erased her look of surprise and replaced it with suspicion. "What's her name?"

Jonas straightened his tie. "What's whose name?"

She laughed and straightened in her seat. "What? We're playing games now?" Patsy shook her head and tsked under her breath. "The annoying thing about you is that you're monogamous. If one woman has captured your heart, the rest of us mortal women don't have a chance. It would be refreshing if life was a romance novel—but in real life, it's just plain silly."

A sardonic laugh rumbled in his chest as he turned back toward the window. "There's no woman."

"Liar."

His gaze swung back to his attorney, but she only shrugged beneath his piercing stare.

"I call them like I see it."

Jonas clenched his jaw tight and remained silent

during the rest of the ride to his office. There were still a few legal issues they needed to go over, but Jonas suggested they review them at another time.

"You're the boss," she said, and remained in the limo to return to her office.

He climbed out and swiftly entered his building.

Once he was alone in the elevator, he finally questioned his reaction—and definitely wondered at Patsy's assessment. Why in the hell didn't he take her up on her offer? He was a free man, despite his affinity for women who belong to other men. In this case his brother.

Who knows, maybe Q was right. Where women are concerned, he needed to keep his heart out of it.

"You have a visitor," Michelle informed him the minute he strolled through the door. "Last minute," she added when he rolled his eyes.

"Give me a minute and then send them on in," he instructed, storming through his office door. Once inside, he made a beeline toward the bar. He only intended to toss back one shot but instead downed three.

At the knock at the door, he bristled, "Come in," and was thrown off guard when Toni Wright stepped into his office. But then, given how his day was going, he shouldn't have been surprised.

"What do you want?" he asked.

"Gee, you don't sound too happy to see me." She closed the door, but inched across the office like she was in pain.

"Are you all right?"

"Yes, of course," she covered, but her tight smile belied the words. "Let's just say that your brother is quite a handful."

Jonas tossed down another shot. "Going well, is it?"

"Too soon to tell."

"Apparently it's not too soon for some things."

Toni stopped and whipped a curious look in his direction. "What is that supposed to mean?"

"You tell me," he said, his gaze still laser-sharp.

"I have no idea." She eased into a vacant chair and sighed in relief to be off her feet. "But to answer your question I'm here on more business."

Jonas didn't want to talk about business. "You know, Sterling is a good guy," he said, unsure where he was going with this. On one hand he loved his brother and on the other…it was like Tracy Mathis all over again. Why that was so, he didn't want to explore.

She smiled. "I know he's a good guy. That's why I agreed to go out with him." Then her eyes took on a teasing glint. "I'll be easy on him."

Jonas poured another drink, while his gaze zeroed in on her long shapely legs. A half a heartbeat later, he had a throbbing hard-on.

Damn it.

"You're being sued," she informed him, reaching into her briefcase.

"I know. You already told me. I've met with—"

"No. I mean, two more women have filed suits."

"What?" Jonas slapped his glass down on the bar. "You have to be kidding me."

"I told you. I don't kid about such things."

What the hell had he gotten himself into by tying himself to T&B Entertainment? He had ownership in the business for six weeks and there was a potential hemorrhage of money.

"How much?"

"The new number is three million."

"Jesus." He poured another drink.

Toni frowned as he brought the glass up to his lips.

"What?" he asked.

"Nothing. I was just wondering...nothing."

Jonas looked down at his drink and then set it back on the bar. "You were just wondering what?"

Toni quickly tossed up her hands. "Forget it. It's none of my business."

Suspicious and then angered by her possible judgment, he marched from around the bar and then realized his mistake when the beautiful attorney emitted a small gasp at his enormous hard-on.

Instead of being embarrassed this time, Jonas slowed his gait to a leisurely stroll.

"You know, I'm starting to think your constant hard-on is a medical condition and has absolutely nothing to do with me," she said.

Jonas took his seat behind the desk. "Then you would be mistaken."

Her brows arched in surprise. "In that case, I'm flattered."

His head cocked with a silly grin. "C'mon. You have to know your effect on men. Especially since I'm surrounded by ex-boyfriends."

Her smile vanished.

"Brian Olson," he said. "Charming man—though I have to admit, he doesn't quite seem like your type."

"And you know my type, do you?"

His gaze leveled with hers. "I think so."

"This I have to hear," she said, crossing her arms and settling back into her chair. "Please, Mr. Hinton. Tell me my type."

"I'm your type," he said simply, and then looked equally surprised he'd said it.

After an awkward silence, Toni burst out laughing. "That's quite an ego you got there."

"Tell me I'm wrong."

"And end your dreams of grandeur?" she bristled. "I couldn't do that."

Jonas's rich laughter overpowered hers. "You're a slippery fish, Ms. Wright."

"One you're sorry you let get away?" she challenged, and then smiled in triumph when his laughter died. After all, to admit that would be a betrayal to his brother. She watched him shift restlessly in his chair for a moment before letting him off the hook.

"The three million is on the table until Friday." She pulled out a set of papers from her briefcase and tossed them across his desk.

He didn't bother to look at them.

"I think the women have a strong case. One, Georgina Wilson, has even recorded some of the incidents. Real entertaining stuff."

"Yes," Jonas said suddenly.

Toni cocked her head. "Yes what?"

"Yes, I'm sorry I let you get away."

William Bassett made his million in real estate. Though he was no Donald Trump, it didn't stop him from living a life of excess. A loud, wise-cracking philanderer, Uncle Willy had long been Solomon's favorite relative.

"What do you mean Nora's suing you? I gave little ma'am the ride of her life. The girl is a tiger in bed…a pussycat on top of the kitchen table and a beast in—"

"We got it, Uncle Willy," Solomon erupted.

"You want to check her out in action? I think I have a few tapes around here somewhere."

"No." Sol jumped in. "That won't be necessary."

"Uncle Willy," Marcel started. "This is serious. Our attorney is actually saying she may have a case." He turned his accusing glare back to his partner. "I warned you this day would come."

"I know. I know." Solomon drew a deep breath. "Uncle Willy, we met with our new partner and—"

"Yeah. I heard. Jonas Hinton. I guess he didn't let bygones be bygones, eh?"

"Anyway," Solomon continued, "we wrapped up one meeting this morning with our attorney—only for him to call us an hour later and tell us two more women are filing suits."

"This is going to set off a chain reaction," Marcel groaned. "And with a staff that's over ninety percent women, this could be a catastrophe."

"Relax, relax." Willy reached across his office

desk to grab his cigar box. "Have a puff. The best Cuba has to offer. Just don't ask me how I got them."

"We didn't come for a smoke," Solomon said, his patience wire-thin.

"Then don't mind me if I do."

Marcel tossed up his hands and then collapsed into a leather chair.

"First of all. I think you guys need to get better legal representation. Nora's suit wouldn't stand. Her being fired had nothing to do with me, right?"

"No," Solomon and Marcel said.

"She's just a gold digger looking to strike gold wherever she can. I'm sure the other two women if you investigate are likely Georgina Wilson and Theodora Golden."

Marcel and Solomon shared another wearied look.

"And how would you know that?"

"Because we all did a foursome."

"A foursome?" Marcel asked.

Willy shrugged. "Why settle for two when you can have three or four? You want to watch? I think I have that tape around here, too...."

Chapter 12

Sterling was having a good day. It was just lunchtime and he'd already closed on a real-estate deal and two of his major investment companies had reported record profits and were expected to close with record highs on the DOW. The only hiccup on his schedule was to meet with his freeloading younger brother for lunch.

"Sterling, my man. I was just beginning to think you were going to stand me up."

"And let my baby brother starve? I wouldn't dream of it."

"Glad to hear it." Quentin stood from the bar and followed his brother and hostess to a vacant table. The brothers kept the chitchat light until Q approached Sterling's latest relationship with Toni Wright.

"So how are things going with you two?"

Sterling's gaze immediately turned suspicious. "Why do you ask?"

"Relax. I'm not interested in stealing your girl."

"Not that you could."

Q's grin sloped lopsidedly. "Of course I could, don't be ridiculous."

Sterling's brows arched. "Not all women like broke, pretty boys to spoil."

"You keep telling yourself that, bro."

Sterling rolled his eyes, and then paused long enough to give their waitress their drink order. "To answer your question, things are going well."

"See a future with her?"

Sterling stiffened in his chair. "Why?"

Quentin shrugged, trying his best to look indifferent. "No reason."

"Do I look like I was born yesterday?"

"Is that a trick question?"

"Q," Sterling said bitingly. "What's with all the questions about Toni and me?" he asked and then warned, "And don't give me that 'no reason' crap."

The brothers' gazes locked for a long moment and then Quentin finally gave up the ghost. "I just noticed how Jonas reacted to your date that day at lunch. He hasn't admitted it, but I think he may have feelings for your girl."

Sterling clamped his jaw shut just as his drink order was delivered to the table.

"You noticed, too," Q said.

"She said nothing was going on between them."

"And you bought that?" Q chuckled. "In that case, I have some swamp land in Florida I'm dying to get off my hands."

Sterling glowered.

"C'mon. You just met the girl. You're not going to tell me you're in love already."

"I didn't say that…but I am attracted to her."

Q shrugged again. "I can see that. She's beautiful. But you know what they say about that."

"The beautiful ones hurt you every time?"

"Straight from the gospel of Prince."

"Well, there you go."

While Sterling sulked in his chair, Q studied him. "It's not that I care one way or the other. I just thought that it's rather encouraging to see Jonas finally showing interest in another woman. Hell, I was beginning to think he would never get over Ophelia."

Sterling nodded, thinking.

"But," Q continued, shrugging, "if you like her, too…"

Toni wasn't rendered speechless often, and in this instance, she feared she would never recover. It wasn't that she'd never been in a position where a man admitted his attraction. Hell, she had men proclaim their undying love and devotion, but none of them had been able to cause the earth to shift beneath her feet.

And though she was seated comfortably in a chair, she felt off centered, overwhelmed and even frightened.

That didn't make sense.

"You have nothing to say?" Jonas asked.

Toni cleared her throat. "What would you like for me to say?"

He slowly cocked his head to the side and studied her. "I'd like to hear what you're thinking."

She shifted in her chair, hoping to right the world beneath her feet. "I'm not sure what I'm thinking." She tried to sound caviler, but wasn't sure it was working. "Truth of the matter is we hardly know each other."

"That's easily rectified."

"And what about your brother?"

Jonas's gaze dropped for several seconds. "I could talk to him."

"You'd do that for little ole me?" she asked, exaggerating her southern lilt.

His gaze snapped back up. Was she teasing him—playing games?

The power ball slammed back into Toni's court. "You know, I'm starting to think you're only attracted to women who are already spoken for." She watched his jawline twitch. "Do you consider me a challenge?"

"Never mind. I've mistaken the attraction to be mutual."

"Oh, I'm attracted to you," she clarified. "Just as I was months ago."

"I wasn't ready…to start dating—then."

"And you are now?"

He shrugged, not liking feeling vulnerable. He

was still recovering from the last time he'd left himself open for a woman.

Toni huffed and rolled her eyes. "I'm not into a lot of head games, Mr. Hinton." She sat up. "My clients are willing to settle for three million."

"And the people in hell want iced water."

"Is that a no, Mr. Hinton?"

"You bet your ass it is," he snapped, and then swiveled his chair around to stare out of his office window. Maybe if he stopped looking at her it would soften his aching erection.

"Don't you think you should discuss this with your partners?"

"No."

He listened as she climbed out of her chair, but instead of her marching toward the door, she approached him from behind.

"I'm going to forget you said that since you're obviously talking out of anger instead of common sense."

Damn, did she have to purr when she talked? When her hand landed softly against his shoulder, he bolted out of his chair as if he'd been shot.

Toni jumped back, surprised.

Belatedly, he realized he'd overreacted, but it was too late to shift control back into his court. "This meeting is over, Ms. Wright."

"Is something wrong, Jonas?" she asked as she stalked forward, her gait still a bit slow. "You seem edgy."

For every step she took, Jonas retreated.

"You know, you're an interesting man, Mr. Hinton. You talk a good game, but when it's time to play, you back away." She cocked her head again. "Curious about the fire, but afraid of getting burned?"

Jonas's head jerked up, giving himself away.

Toni stopped, stunned that she had guessed it right. "You're afraid that if something happens between us, you'll get burned?"

"No," he croaked.

But both knew it was a lie.

"Why didn't you call me when I was in California?" she asked, stalking again.

This time, Jonas stood firm. "I was busy."

"Bullshit."

He cocked his head. "Maybe I wasn't sure I was interested."

"Bullshit." She stopped when her breasts brushed against his chest and then watched his reaction.

And there was a reaction.

A spark flared in his eyes, his jaw tightened and a jolt of electricity bolted through their compressed chests.

Toni stoked the flames by sliding her hand up his chest. "It's time to get back into the game, Jonas. Play with a little fire." Sliding on a grin, she leaned forward and did what she should have done six months ago: kissed him.

And what a kiss.

The previous bolt of electricity was nothing compared to the glorious inferno roaring into her veins the moment their lips connected. Her bones melted within her skin and she had no choice but to slack limp against him—successfully handing the power ball back over.

Meanwhile, Jonas had never felt more alive in his life. Her soft lips and teasing tongue unleashed an animal he'd long thought had died. He deepened the kiss, widening her lips for the exploratory stroke of his tongue. His hands slid into her thick hair and his mouth slanted over hers in a hungry demand.

The kiss was not unlike a vampire's bite, draining all he could: her soul, her essence. He selfishly wanted it all.

During his tightening embrace, Toni found it difficult to string two cohesive thoughts together. The lesson when one played with fire: you never know who will be burned by the flames.

Jonas backed away from the office wall, wrapped an arm around her waist and directed her toward his desk. This time, he did sweep everything to the floor so that he could press her body down on top of it.

Their delicious kiss continued while each tugged at the other's clothes. Neither thought about the consequences of their actions. All that mattered was this moment—and sating a curiosity and satisfying their bodies' growing hunger.

Jonas's door bolted open.

Michelle's voice floated into the office. "Jonas, your— Oh, my God!" She jumped and covered her eyes. "I'm sorry. I'm…" she said, backing out of the room. "I'll reschedule."

When the door slammed closed behind his embarrassed assistant, Jonas and Toni looked at each other and burst out laughing.

"I really need to start locking that door."

"Obviously." Toni glanced down, surprised to see a breast popped out of her lace bra. She glanced back up with a mischievous grin and was surprised to see Jonas was already climbing off the desk.

"I'm sorry," he said. "I don't know what came over me."

"I do," she said, sitting up and reaching for him in an attempt to reclaim the moment; however, Jonas backed away.

"Please accept my apologies, Ms. Wright. This should have never happened and it won't happen again."

"C'mon. We've talked about this. I'm not going to hurt you. I'm not Ophelia."

The moment she'd said the name, she regretted it. She might as well have slammed a steel door between them.

"Your offer…as well as the three-million-dollar settlement request…is rejected."

Toni's mouth fell open. "You think I did this—" She glanced down at her exposed body and then stabbed him with an angry glare "—as a way to get you to agree to the settlement?"

His brows arched inquiringly.

"You're a goddamn bastard." She pushed herself from off the desk and slid her breast back into her bra. "I don't know why the hell I thought I cared about you."

Hurt flashed across his features, but Jonas quickly turned away with a curse.

Toni hastily rebuttoned her blouse and grabbed her briefcase. "I'll see you in court, asshole!"

Jonas remained staring out the window until the door slammed and the walls rattled around him. When he finally collapsed into his chair, he felt like every bit the asshole she'd called him.

Chapter 13

"It's not you. It's me," Toni said, clutching Sterling's hands while they huddled together at the ESPN Zone. On the hundreds of televisions screens around them, the Atlanta Braves had just taken the lead at the bottom of the fifth inning.

Sterling tried to pull his hand away. "It's you or is it Jonas?" he questioned softly.

"I told you before—there's nothing going on between me and your brother." Guilt burned at the tips of her ears, however, she was fairly certain Sterling couldn't see that; but when their gazes met, she had second thoughts. "I like you," she admitted. "But not in the way that you want."

He nodded, took a swig of his beer.

She waited, not sure how he would react to her rehearsed speech. A part of her was prepared for an explosion or some kind of verbal attack, especially if Jonas had already confessed what had transpired in his office last week, but instead Sterling looked remarkably blasé.

"That's too bad."

For a moment she thought she needed to clean her ears out. "Excuse me?"

"Don't get me wrong, I regret things didn't work out, but…at the same time I sort of sensed or rather I was told that Jonas is more than a little interested in you."

"Oh, he is?" She laughed and then reached for her own beer. "Did he tell you this?"

"No. Quentin did."

"And he gets his information from…"

Sterling shrugged. "He said that it was rather obvious."

I thought it was obvious, too.

"Well, your brother is wrong."

Sterling weighed her words and reached for his beer again. "It wouldn't be the first time but…I guess I was sort of hoping he wasn't. After all Jonas has been through I find it encouraging he's finally interested in someone new."

Toni turned her attention to one of the large television screens. Anything was better than discussing Jonas Hinton. It had been a week since that humiliating scene in his office and she was just as angry now as she was when she'd stormed out.

"What about you?" Sterling asked, suddenly.

"What about me?"

Sterling shifted and leaned forward in his chair. "How do you feel about my older brother?"

"I told you, there's nothing—"

"Yes. Yes. There's nothing going on between you two. I heard you. But that's not what I asked you. How do you *feel* about him?"

"There's nothing to feel," she lied smoothly. "I hardly know him. We met once waiting for a plane and the other two times I've seen him were strictly for business." She tried to meet Sterling's gaze, but found it difficult since his eyes were so similar to his older brother.

"I understand," he finally said. "It's probably difficult to discuss this with me."

Guess that meant he saw straight through that line of bs she'd just given him.

"Well, I hope you'll forgive me for what I did tonight. Or rather what I'm about to do."

Toni froze as her eyes narrowed suspiciously. "What are you about to do?"

Just then, popping up like a jack-in-a-box, Jonas appeared at their table. "I thought you said tonight was boys' night out?" His hand dropped onto Sterling's shoulder with a loud whack.

Toni's gaze shot up as a firestorm of emotions blazed through her. The only problem was that one half was happy to see him while the other half still wanted to maim or at least throttle him.

"Sorry, man," Sterling said casually. "I didn't think you'd mind if I invited my new girlfriend along."

The blatant lie surprised Toni and when she looked back down at Sterling, he was actually grinning. This was an odd way to play matchmaker—especially if she was supposed to be his date.

She shook her head, not sure she wanted to play this game. Jonas Hinton's emotional baggage was larger than she'd originally thought and as far as she was concerned, life was too short for this kind of drama.

"Are you going to pull up a chair or are you going to stand there all night?" Sterling asked Jonas.

Determined to show she didn't give a damn whether he stayed or let the door hit him where the good Lord split him, Toni rolled her eyes back toward one of the television screens and sulked with her beer.

She heard a chair scrape the floor and then the loud rustling as Jonas took his seat. "Where's Q?"

"Something came up."

During the ensuing silence, Toni became conscience of Jonas's heavy stare, but she remained steadfast in her resolve to ignore him.

"I'm going to head up to the bar and order us some wings. Can I get anyone anything else?"

Toni shook her head and watched as a Pittsburgh Pirate struck out and ended the top of the sixth inning.

"I'll have a beer," Jonas said.

"I'll be right back," Sterling said, leaving the table.

"Giving up the hard stuff?" she snipped, but then wanted to kick herself for speaking.

"No, *Mom*. I plan on hitting the bottle later to-night. Something tells me that I'm going to need it."

Her gaze turned away from the TV to impale him. "Screw you."

Their eyes locked and Jonas wrestled with the apology poised on the tip of his tongue. He didn't want to feel the things he felt whenever he was around her. Even now, with her once again dressed down in a pair of jeans and an Atlanta Braves T-shirt, his cock was throbbing painfully against his leg like he was some prepubescent teenager with his first crush.

Why did he find everything about her so... perfect? Her warm chocolate skin, her thick shoulder-length hair, he now knew to be soft and silky straight. And that wasn't counting things he shouldn't know, like how good she tasted and how wonderful the weight of her breast felt in his hand.

"Mr. Hinton," she said softly.

"Yes?"

"You're staring."

He blinked out of his stupor and refrained from cursing under his breath.

Meanwhile, Toni settled back into her chair as if she was the cat's meow. Her anger waned as her dark gaze flickered with triumph. "You're going to go down fighting, aren't you?"

"I don't know what you're talking about," he lied, and then glanced over his shoulder. *How long did it take to place an order?*

"You want me, but you don't want to want me."

"You're with my brother."

"You didn't seem to care about that when you were ripping my clothes off last week."

"What? You think we're going to share you or something?"

"Ooh." Her eyes lit merrily. "A Hinton sandwich? That sounds like fun."

Red waves of anger darkened Jonas's honey complexion. "I don't share," he said through gritted teeth.

Satisfied in successfully goading him, Toni gave a casual shrug and returned to feigning interest in the baseball game surrounding them.

"One beer," Sterling announced, setting a Corona before his brother. "Our hot wings are on its way."

"Yippee," Jonas mumbled.

"Look, you know, maybe this really should be a boys' night out," Toni said, standing. Whatever attraction she thought she felt for Jonas, she was definitely no longer interested in pursuing. Suppressed bad boy or not, life was too short.

"No, wait." Sterling stood, as well, and then his cell phone rang on his hip. "Don't go." The phone rang again. "Hold on, let me just take this call."

Toni exhaled and sat back in her chair.

"Sterling here." He held up a finger and moved away from the table, leaving her, once again, with Jonas.

Toni no longer pretended to be interested in the game and instead, kept glancing at her watch. Occasionally, her eyes would dart to Jonas to confirm he was still studying her.

She tried her best not to be turned on by his

broodiness, but that was growing harder the longer she remained at the table. Where did Sterling go? Maybe she should take a cab, but then she doubted whether she had cash in her purse.

She looked around the sports bar again. *Where in the hell is he?*

"Do I make you nervous, Ms. Wright?" he asked, mocking.

"You?" She laughed. "A man who's afraid of fire? Hardly."

His lips curved into a devastating smile and Toni was angered that her pulse quickened beneath his darkening gaze.

"You're sooo sure you have me figured out."

Settling back against her seat, Toni lazily crossed her arms. "I can read you like a book. My only mistake was that I initially thought you were at least an interesting book."

Jonas's dimples deepened at the jibe and a low laugh rumbled within his chest. "Well, I can't say the same thing about you, Ms. Wright. You are, indeed, an interesting book."

"Think you know me, do you?"

He shook his head, but his gaze remained steady. "I'm trying not to presume anything. After all, you told me very little of yourself that day in the airport."

That was true, she realized. She walked away knowing about one of the most painful events in his life and she left him with nothing more than a business card.

"If you'd called, I would have been happy to fill in the blanks."

"It always comes down to that," he said, lowering his gaze to his beer bottle for a few seconds. "I did call once," he admitted.

Toni blinked in surprise, but then grew cautious on whether to believe his claim. "It was the next day actually. I reached your office voice mail…and simply hung up."

"Why didn't you leave a message?"

He shrugged and fell silent for a long moment. "Long-distance relationships are not my thing."

"You seem to be into very little."

"I'm not into pilfering my brother's girlfriend, if that's what you mean."

"I'm not his girlfriend."

"What? This is a casual fling for you?"

Toni's eyes narrowed. "What are you insinuating?"

"Nothing. I mean, I did come home and hear you two in the den. Sounded to me like you were really into each other."

"The den?" she asked. "What the hell are you talking about?"

A cell phone chirped just as a waitress appeared and dropped off a basket of hot wings.

Jonas and Toni both reached for their phones.

"It's mine," Jonas said, and then frowned when he recognized the number. "It's Sterling."

Toni closed her eyes and dropped her face into the palms of her hands. "He wouldn't," she whispered.

"Where are you, bro?" Jonas asked the moment he answered the phone.

"Sorry, man," Sterling said. "Something's come up. Can you do me a favor and make sure Toni gets home?"

"Well, I, uh, really don't think that's such a good idea."

"Thanks, man. I'll really owe you one."

"But—"

"Plus, things were getting a little awkward since she dumped me tonight."

"What?" Jonas's gaze zeroed in on Toni's bowed head.

"Yeah. She was really sweet about it. There's no hard feelings. Well, I have to go. Thanks for doing this. I owe you one."

"Wait, Sterl—" There was a click and the sound of dead air.

"He wouldn't. He didn't," Toni continued to recite.

Jonas closed his phone and returned it to his hip. "He did. If I didn't know any better I'd say that we were set up," Jonas said, reaching into the basket of hot wings.

"Wow. I see why you're so successful. No one can pull anything over your eyes." She stood. "Good night. It's been real…interesting."

Jonas shot out a hand and caught her by the wrist before she could take a step. "Where are you going?"

"Limited intelligence, I see." She smiled benignly and tried to pull her hand from his grasp. "I'm going home and, if it's not too late, find better company for the evening."

His grip tightened. "Like Brian Olson?"

She lifted an inquisitive brow. "He's certainly a possibility."

The hard glint in his eyes weakened Toni's knees and made it damn hard for her to remind herself that she didn't want any part of his drama.

"Stay here. I'll be your date for the evening."

"I said *better* company." She challenged him head-on. "Someone who knows what they want and goes after it."

They stood in what seemed like a stalemate before he finally released her hand and ordered her to, "Sit down."

"Excuse me?"

"I said sit down." He reached for his beer. "I'll take you home tonight—after we eat."

Toni couldn't believe she was actually considering sitting back down, but there was something about his sudden take-charge attitude that had piqued her curiosity.

Jonas pushed back the chair beside him with his foot. "Sit."

She sat.

"Eat."

Toni rolled her eyes. "Jonas—"

"I want you," he said, successfully shutting her up. "I just don't know whether I can have you and then walk away." He leaned forward. "And I need to be able to walk away."

As Toni held his stare, a million images raced

through her mind. All of them involved naked bodies, sweat and a great deal of Gatorade. "In that case, I think that can be arranged."

Grown folks' business…

Chapter 14

Rapt in Toni's versions of events, Alyssa wondered why the bride had stopped talking. Then she slowly became aware that all eyes were on her.

"What? Did I do something wrong?"

Toni smiled and gathered up her dress so that she could glide over to her. "No, sweetheart. You haven't done anything wrong." She slid an arm around Alyssa's thin shoulders. "It's just that, uh, some of this story isn't fit for young ears."

The bridesmaids snickered softly behind them and Toni softened the blow by pinching Alyssa's apple cheeks.

"You mean, that you want to talk about sex?" Alyssa asked.

"Well," Toni looked around while her face darkened abruptly. "Something like that."

Alyssa's shoulders deflated as she dropped her head dramatically in hopes to convince everyone to let her stay. When no one said a word, but instead let her cross the room slower than a turtle, she decided to offer a suggestion.

"You could always skip over the sex part."

"Not if she knows what's good for her," Ashley quipped.

"I know that's right," Maria agreed.

Brooklyn shook her head at her friends. "Behave."

"I'm sorry," Toni said again, this time poking out her bottom lip.

Defeated, Alyssa turned and walked out of the door. The minute she closed the door, peals of laughter erupted on the other side. "I can't wait until I grow up."

Another trickle of laughter slipped under the door, tempting Alyssa to press her ear against it to see if she could hear the rest of the story.

"Whatcha doing, Alice?"

Alyssa jumped and twirled away from the door. At the sight of her future husband strolling down the hallway, the muscles in her throat tightened and made it impossible for her to speak.

Stopping in front of her, Quentin laughed and shook his head. "You know, there's no need for you to be shy around me. You've been living here at my parents' home your whole life. We're practically family."

His words caused a world of butterflies to flutter madly in the pit of her stomach. She wanted to be a part of his family, all right—the part that would marry him and give him at least a dozen babies that looked just like him.

The women laughed again, and their melodic sound caught Q's ear. This time, he pressed his ear against the door but then winked down at her. A second later, he pulled away with a knowing smile.

"Oh, this isn't fit for young ears," he said, planting his hands on her shoulders and turning her away from the door. Alyssa sensed that if she wasn't there, he would have been more tempted to hang around and listen.

"We better find you something else to do," he said, laughing and directing her down the hallway. "If your father knew you were listening to that kind of stuff—"

"I wasn't," she said, finding her voice.

Q laughed. "Ah, so you do speak."

They reached the staircase and Alyssa's panic increased when she saw her father rushing around with the servers.

"Really," she insisted. "I just wanted to hear how the bride and groom fell in love. I didn't hear anything bad. Please don't tell my dad." She turned and glanced up at Quentin. "Please."

"Alyssa?" her father called.

She turned and smiled down at him. "Hey, Dad."

"Is there a problem?" His suspicious gaze darted from her to Quentin.

"No, sir. I just finished helping the bride and the bridesmaids."

Alfred nodded, but his eyes remained locked on the youngest Hinton. "All right, then. You go on to your room and try to stay out of the way."

"Yes, sir." She started down the staircase, but relaxed when she heard Q's soft whisper.

"Don't worry. It will be our little secret."

Meanwhile, back in the bride's suite, Toni recaptured her friends' attention by telling them when things shifted to another level between her and Jonas.

"Believe it or not, it happened the same night I decided to end things with Sterling...."

Chapter 15

Toni never pictured Jonas as a motorcycle kind of guy. So when he escorted her to the red-and-black Harley-Davidson parked in the ESPN Zone's parking deck, she literally had to do a double take. "You've got to be kidding me," she said.

Jonas cocked a half grin and swung his leg over the sexy sleek bike. "You said you wanted a wild ride, didn't you?"

She laughed and settled her hands on her hips. "I wasn't talking about a bike and you know it."

"Then consider it a warm-up." He winked. "Climb on."

"I don't have a helmet."

"Here. You can use mine."

Hesitating, she met his challenging gaze and then swung her leg around the steel and chrome and slid her head into the helmet. The moment the machine rumbled to life between her legs, a smile curved her lips and her arms wrapped around his waist.

"Damn. I have to get me one of these."

"Hang on," he shouted, kicked up the kickstand and roared off.

Toni discovered there was an inherent attitude when one was on the back of a Harley. One that was dangerous, sexy and rebellious. Within minutes, they were cruising down the highway, scenery whipping past while an incredible vibration hummed through her.

Hell, this was nothing more than a gigantic sex toy as far as she was concerned. The fact that she was hanging on to one hell of a male specimen made the experience more…orgasmic.

The thirty-minute ride to her Alpharetta home flew by entirely too fast and then Jonas parked his bike behind her black Benz on her circular driveway.

Toni's body continued to throb and pulse like a wild heartbeat. Hell, the bike was all the foreplay she needed. After removing her helmet, she wondered whether her quaking legs could stand.

"How did you like your first ride?" Jonas asked.

"I loved it." She sighed and took the risk in pushing herself up off the bike.

"Where are you going?" His strong arm wrapped around her waist and pulled her forward.

Her breasts perked at his continued possessiveness and there was no mistaking that his hidden bad boy had finally decided to come out and play.

Lifting one of her legs, though it was still trembling after their long ride, he placed her back onto the bike—but this time she faced him.

"I thought we were going inside?" she asked.

Jonas ignored the question and pulled her in close for an explosive kiss. His delicious mouth sent a shock of heat coursing through her body. When his tongue invaded, its erotic dance caused an ache between her legs.

She arched against his hard chest, her breasts transmitting tiny jolts of pleasure. Her brain tried to navigate through a thick fog of desire, but soon gave up the fight. She moaned when his strong hands slid beneath her top, roamed up her flat stomach and then cupped her full and sensitive breasts.

When he squeezed, Toni felt herself go wet. After another squeeze, she couldn't believe that she was on the verge of an orgasm.

She still had her clothes on!

That was true for exactly another two seconds. She blinked and Jonas had managed to whip her shirt over her head and unhooked her bra like he was a descendant of Houdini.

You're outside, a small voice shouted from the back of her head. Her house may have been a ways off from the main road, but she was sure her neighbors, at a good angle, would be able to get quite an eyeful.

Before she could give voice to her concern, Jonas leaned her back until she lay against the bike's chromed frame and he tilted forward to graze on her quivering breasts. Each time his tongue lapped at her hardened nipples, it grew harder to control her breathing.

Teeth scraped against her tender flesh and she nearly leaped off the bike. However, Jonas kept her firmly in place and even dared to nip at her breasts again. The next couple of times, she sucked in a painful gasp, but thereafter, his gentle gnawing felt downright pleasurable and she couldn't stop rocking her head and moaning into the heavens.

Emboldened by her response, Jonas's hands descended and pulled at her jeans.

"J-Jonas…my…neighbors…"

"Shh," he said, his breath brushing against her skin. "This is what you wanted, right?"

Toni licked her lips and tried to speak again. "Yes…but—"

"Then we are going to do this *my* way," he rasped, jerking her pants open. "I'm in control. You got that?"

She nodded, but that wasn't what he wanted.

"Let me hear you say it," he commanded softly.

Toni blinked, momentarily confused. Did the man truly think she could concentrate on a word he was saying? However, when his mouth stopped performing its wonderful magic, her mind cleared and she was desperate to return to paradise. "You are in control," she panted, and reached for him.

Jonas sat up, balanced the bike between his legs and lifted hers into the air.

Toni reached for the handlebars in fear that she was going to fall off and end the night with a trip to the emergency room. But once again, Jonas proved that he was quite skillful at getting to what he wanted.

Dressed now in only a pair of heels and a red thong, Toni felt eerily like one of those Budweiser models draped over a Harley. And if her neighbor, Mrs. Baker, looked out her kitchen window, that would be exactly what she'd see.

"God, you have an incredible body," Jonas gasped before he returned to sucking and nibbling on her breasts.

Instantly, Toni's eyes rolled to the back of her head while a stream of moans fell carelessly from her lips. Jonas's hand also returned, but this time it slipped beneath the lacy thong and penetrated her with one and then two fingers.

She was melting. Toni was absolutely certain of it and thought there was no better way to leave this world than melting in the rain.

Rain?

She opened her eyes and sure enough a light drizzle sprinkled across her skin. "J-Jonas?"

He looked up, his mouth still locked on a breast. However, the look he gave said that he was very much aware that it was raining, but that he was still in control and he had every intention of making love to her on his Harley.

"Never mind," she whispered, and lowered her head back down and continued to submit to his every whim to see where they might take her. So far she couldn't complain.

His thumb joined the party between her legs, working her hard clit until she inched higher on the bike. To add to her delight, Jonas's lips abandoned her glistening nipples to descend down her body.

Before she knew it, her legs were back in the air, but this time he gave the command to, "Wrap them around my neck."

She did as she was told and was rewarded when Jonas's magnificently skilled tongue plunged into her and within a couple of strokes a powerful wave hit her and she cried out in abandonment.

Still he continued, sucking and lapping until she shuddered and gasped from a second orgasm.

The night's drizzle morphed into a steady stream and Jonas finally lowered her bottom back onto the bike.

"Sit up."

Again, she followed his orders and was rewarded with another soul-stirring kiss.

"Take my shirt off," he said, his mouth shifting to skim her right earlobe.

"Gladly." Instead of fooling with the buttons, she removed his shirt in the same manner he'd removed her top. She untucked it from his jeans and then lifted it and his T-shirt over his head.

Damn.

Her eyes feasted on his wide, chiseled chest that left no doubt it was obtained by hours of hard work and sweat. The way his beautiful honey complexion glistened in the rain, Toni suffered a severe sweet tooth and thought that she would surely die if she couldn't have at least a small taste.

She leaned forward for a quick kiss and a lick.

Jonas gently pushed her away and glared in reprimand. "Stand up."

Toni stood and Jonas allowed the bike to tilt back onto the kickstand before getting off the bike. Less than a minute later, he was nude and climbing back onto the bike and rolling on a condom.

"How are we going to—"

"Climb onto my lap," he said. "Wrap your legs around my waist."

She stared at him for a moment, wondering if she should trust his engineering skills, but she was too horny to hesitate for long. Climbing onto his lap, almost toppling over a few times, Toni eased down and joined their bodies together with a sigh.

He filled her so completely that he could feel every tremor coursing through her.

"Are you all right?" he asked while waiting for her body to adjust to his size—even though it was sheer torture to be patient.

Panting near his ear, she tried to speak but then abandoned the effort to just nod instead.

The rain had finally turned into a downpour, but the new lovers remained steadfast in their decision to stay outside.

"Okay. In order for us to remain seated, you're going to have to take over for a little while and ride."

"Oh?" she asked, sounding deliciously wicked.

Jonas smiled, not bothered by giving up a little control. He just wished she'd get on with it while he still had some restraint.

The first time she lifted her body and slid back down his throbbing erection, he feared their tricky position would land them on the hard pavement; but he managed to balance most of their weight on his strong legs.

She tried the motion a second time—and then a third and Jonas's body was soaring out of the stratosphere. He felt fevered and more than a little confused over what was happening to him.

He'd suspected being with Toni would be good—but he'd never dreamed it would be this good. Every curve, every muscle welcomed him home. But that didn't make any sense.

A low growl rumbled in the back of his throat when Toni accelerated her speed. He buried his face in her bouncing breasts, while the intoxicating scent of lavender enveloped him.

Toni's panting also quickened while her body tightened around him. He wanted her to come one more time before his own orgasm hit, but whatever restraint he had was long gone and it was now anybody's race.

Thunder rumbled off in the distance. Toni tightened around Jonas like a boa constrictor while still pumping her hips. At last a final scream tore from her throat and her third orgasm slammed into her.

Jonas roared as his body went rigid and her shuddering passage milked him dry. At last, his trembling legs gave out and they tumbled over onto the paved driveway, laughing.

Chapter 16

By the next morning, Toni was exhausted and every muscle in her body rebelled in protest. Even now while lying in bed, her left leg twitched as though it had blown a circuit. And yet, each time Jonas reached for her, the protest ended and her body welcomed him.

She'd never been with a man with such stamina and one who introduced her to so many new positions. To say that the sex was mind-blowing would be an understatement and to say that their wild coupling was just that—would be a lie.

At least, he'd finally allowed her a couple of hours to get some sleep. When she woke, the sun warmed her naked body and the heavenly aroma of fresh coffee drifted on the air.

Smiling, she tried to stretch, but those damn sore muscles threatened to kill her on the spot.

"I see you're finally up." Jonas chuckled, walking into the bedroom nude and carrying two steaming coffee mugs. "I hope you don't mind, but I invaded the kitchen and made us some coffee."

Wincing, Toni fought all that was holy to sit up and accept her morning fuel. "Thank you," she said, and smiled when his gaze zeroed in on her exposed breasts. Judging by the look in his eyes, her mini break was nearing an end.

God help her.

However as he walked around to the other side of the bed, Toni's eyes were drawn to his strong physique and his impressive package. The man needed to be sculpted or photographed so he could be admired by all womankind.

The bed dipped beneath his weight when he settled in beside her and took his first sip of his coffee. "Is it all right?" he asked. "I guessed on how you'd like it."

"It's perfect," she said, enjoying the way the hot liquid warmed her body. "I'll be lucky if I don't catch my death for playing out in the rain last night."

Jonas's eyes held a mischievous glint as they cut toward her. "It's still raining. I thought we could play some more out there."

She quirked a brow. "You love the threat of getting caught?"

"You don't?"

He had her there and he knew it. Falling into an

amused silence, Toni watched Jonas from the corner of her eyes while continuing to sip from her coffee. Flashes of last night played across her mind and a familiar tingle pulsed at her core.

Good heavens, the man had made her insatiable. She could think of nothing but the power of his body enfolding her and taking her places she'd only dreamed of.

Why was it that he looked at home, lying next to her?

Minutes later, Jonas set his cup aside and then curled toward her to fondle her firm breasts. The tingling and pulsing intensified.

"Tell me more about yourself," he whispered before sliding his tongue across her nipples.

To be safe, she set her own cup aside. "What do you want to know?"

Jonas shrugged lazily. "I don't know. Where are you from?"

"Right here. I'm a Georgia Peach. A Grady baby."

"You were born at Grady Hospital?"

She nodded. "Yep."

"What about your parents?"

Toni shifted uncomfortably. "What about them?"

"Are they alive?"

She swallowed. "No."

Jonas stopped his gentle lapping and pulled away from her. "I'm so sorry."

"Don't be." She smiled, but her voice sounded pained. "It was a long time ago."

"What happened?"

Toni's gaze avoided his by darting toward the rain-splattered window. Suddenly, the room grew cold while she contemplated telling her standard lie—her parents were killed in a car accident—versus the truth: her father killed her mother and then himself when she tried to leave him.

"Toni?"

"Car accident," she answered in a broken whisper.

"I'm so sorry for your loss." He pulled her close. "Do you have any living relatives?"

"Not a one."

Jonas kissed her. "Talk about opposites," Jonas murmured. "I have family members crawling out of the woodwork. My father was the youngest of ten."

Toni pulled back from the waves of depression to glance at him. "Really?"

"Literally hundreds of cousins. I swear, I've met most of them because they wanted me or my family to invest in one crazy-hair scheme or another."

"Still. It must be nice having a big family."

He thought it over and nodded. "Yeah. It is."

Jonas was surprised by the sudden gloss in Toni's eyes, mainly because she'd always been so good in pretending nothing ever got to her.

Instead of pawing at her or hiking her legs around his waist, like he wanted to do, Jonas just let his fingers glide down her belly while he continued asking questions. "Why did you become a lawyer?"

Toni didn't answer. She just watched as his finger made lazy circles around her belly button.

"Toni?" he asked, wondering if she'd heard him.

"My father always thought that it would be a great out," she whispered. "Back then, people thought if you were either a doctor or a lawyer then you were set for life." She chuckled. "He didn't want his children to continue the cycle of living paycheck to paycheck or tumbling into the system. The ghetto—the projects—or whatever it's being called nowadays." Her eyes became dreamy as she recalled the past.

"I didn't want to become a lawyer. I thought I was going to become the next Diana Ross or Donna Summer."

Jonas cocked his head, but stopped himself from asking the one question a man should *never* ask.

"Forty-three," she answered with a wink.

His head performed the quick math.

"What? Too old?" she asked, preparing for the rejection.

"Are you kidding me?" He laughed, snuggling close. "Do you know how cool this will make me on the playground?"

Toni laughed and loved it when he rewarded her with a kiss. Surely, there wasn't a softer pair of lips on the planet and none that ever made her feel as though she was floating on clouds.

Jonas slipped his hands around her and then rolled onto his back, pulling her to lie on top of him. "Look at there. Your favorite position," he whispered.

She smiled and returned to kissing his addictive lips while cradling his head in her hands.

Jonas's hands slid from her waist to cup her apple-shaped behind and gave it a squeeze. It had been a long time since he had felt so free and relaxed around another woman.

But don't get too close, the small voice in his head warned. Right behind that, Quentin's motto looped in his head. *When it comes to women, keep your heart out of it.*

Jonas tensed.

Toni's eyes fluttered open. Something happened. She stared into Jonas's clear brown eyes, trying to figure it out. "What is it?" she asked.

"What?" he asked, and carved out an innocent smile.

Then she saw it. He was trying to distance his emotions. This was just sex, after all; something that he could walk away from.

She smiled—almost laughed when she realized why she'd recognized the shift. How many times had she pulled this same maneuver? "Relax," she said, rolling off of him. "I haven't forgotten our deal."

Shaking her head, she climbed out of bed and headed toward the bathroom.

"Wait. Where are you going?" he asked, sitting up.

"I'm going to take a shower," she answered casually and refused to look back. "I'm sure you know how to let yourself out." Toni kept her head high, but just barely managed to make it inside the bathroom and closed the door before tears leaped from her eyes.

Next, she turned the shower on to full blast and

then submerged herself beneath the steady stream of hot water. Still, she could feel the tears running down her face.

What in the hell is wrong with me?

How long had she practiced protecting her heart? Hell, she was expert in not getting too close. But… something was different this time. Jonas was different.

Or was he?

At this point, she didn't know if that was true or if it was wishful thinking. Either way, maybe it was best that she stayed away from him. She corked her tears and nodded at the decision.

After all, she'd gotten what she wanted: a nice tumble in the sack…and even on a bike. Toni was also convinced she had even helped him in his heartbreak recovery.

By the time she'd finished washing her body to reach for the shampoo, she was feeling a lot like her former self.

Jonas was more than bothered by the way Toni had dismissed him. Hell, he thought everything was going fine, and then the next thing he knew, she was mad. At least, she seemed mad. He thought about waiting to talk to her, and then he thought about joining her in the shower, but then he realized it was probably best to just go.

He picked up his damp clothes from the bedroom floor and quickly got dressed. He wanted to be gone by the time she got out of the shower. Though it wasn't his first time slipping out of a woman's house in the morning, Jonas felt as though he was doing something wrong.

Not to mention, he really didn't want to go.

"Maybe it's time you invest in seeing a psychiatrist," Quentin said, packing his bags. "I think you have a screw loose or something."

Jonas grumbled under his breath, but thought his youngest brother may be onto something. He was more confused now than he had ever been.

"So how was she?" Q chanced asking.

Jonas's look turned into a scowl.

"I know. I know. You never kiss and tell." Quentin crammed the last of his things in the bag and then struggled to zip it up. "It's really an annoying habit you got," he added. "Me? I have this whole rating system in play. If a girl—"

"Q, please spare me."

"All right, bro. Don't say I've never tried to help out." He laughed. "I was the one who told Sterling to back off so you could have your shot."

Jonas's head snapped up. "You what?"

"Aw. You don't have to thank me." Q pumped up his chest. "The fact that you got laid last night tells me I did my good deed for the year. I expect a good Christmas gift. Cash, if you don't mind."

"I never said that I—"

"You didn't have to." Quentin laughed. "You're glowing like a pregnant woman. Have you looked in the mirror?"

Jonas shook his head and started to leave the room.

"I have to tell you, I'm a little disappointed in you," Quentin tossed at him.

"Come again?"

Q shrugged. "Had I known you were interested in just *sleeping* with Toni, I would have never asked Sterling to back off. I thought you wanted more than that. Guess I was wrong about that. Right?"

Jonas's throat clogged with emotion, but after a moment of hesitation, he managed to croak, "Right."

Chapter 17

Nora Gibson was not happy with her attorney. It had now been two months since she'd filed her lawsuit and she'd banked on having her money in the bank by now, but apparently Marcel, Solomon and their new partner liked to play hardball. Hardball meant she would have to go to court.

"Maybe we should lower the offer," Nora suggested, looking over at her friends Georgina and Theodora. "Say 1.5 million?"

The women's gazes scattered among themselves before they nodded like a trio of bobble-heads.

Toni's hackles rose as she sensed trouble. "Why should we do that?" she asked, focusing on the Prada-clad ringleader. "The tapes are our ace in the hole. When the jury hears William Bassett's inappropriate propositions at the workplace and reads the complaints filed with T&B Human Resources department—this is a done deal. There's no way we can lose."

She glanced around at the women, half expecting them to be inspired by her short speech, but the energy in the room didn't quite feel right. "Is there something you ladies aren't telling me?"

Anther round of nervous looks ensued before Nora piped up with a, "No. Of course not."

Toni's eyes narrowed as she attempted to crack the women into a confession, but the women pursed their lips and remained united.

"All right. Then we proceed forward?"

"Offer the 1.5 million," Nora said firmly. "And let them know that it's a good deal. A damn good deal."

After her clients left her office, Toni was forced to reevaluate the whole case. No doubt about it, her clients were holding out on her and she couldn't afford for her first major case to blow up in her face.

She groaned. It's never a good strategy to lower an asking price. A man like Jonas Hinton would know that.

Not to mention, she had hoped for a little more time before she had to see Jonas again; time to get her game face back on.

It had nearly been a week since their wild Harley ride and truth be told, every time she passed a biker on the streets she couldn't help but remember the strong vibrations humming between her legs—and that had nothing to do with the Harley.

Almost a week—and no phone call.

Drawing in a deep breath, Toni reminded herself she'd promised Jonas there were no strings attached. But that didn't mean he had permission to avoid common courtesy and *not* call.

Right?

Slumping back in her chair, Toni glared at the phone for a full minute. "What am I doing?" she asked herself. "I don't care if he calls. I have a life. There are plenty of men who…who are waiting for *me* to call them."

Toni nodded, agreeing with herself. "The hell with Jonas Hinton."

The phone rang and she jumped to answer it. "Hello."

"Guess who."

Frowning into the hand unit, she knew one thing: the caller wasn't Jonas. "Um…"

"Brian," the caller supplied.

"Brian?" she repeated, momentarily confused.

"Don't tell me you forgot about me already," he joked.

Her memory clicked back on and she finally remembered her ex-boyfriend. "Of course I remember you," she covered, laughing. "Can't a girl play hard to get?"

"Then you are definitely a master at the game."

Two minutes on the phone with Brian and Toni's confidence restored itself. She was in control and flirting wildly. She even agreed to meet him for drinks for happy hour.

"I look forward to seeing you again," Brian concluded. "Who knows—maybe we'll even pick up where we left off?"

Toni shrugged with a smile. "Yeah. Who knows?"

Startled silence greeted Jonas the moment he entered the main conference room at T&B Entertainment. All eyes followed him as he walked toward the head of the table where Marcel and Solomon perched.

"I guess I missed the memo regarding this morning's staff meeting." He glanced down at one of the attractive staff members. "Do you mind?"

"Not at all, Mr. Hinton." She stood and offered him her chair.

"Thank you." He eased into the comfortable leather chair while smiling at his two partners. "I hope I didn't miss much."

Marcel and Solomon looked as though they wanted to leap at his neck.

"Not much at all," Marcel seethed. "We are discussing possible new artists and artists' development strategies. You know, things you don't know anything about."

A few nervous titters erupted around the room.

"One thing you'll learn about me, Mr. Taylor, is that I'm always happy to learn." He turned away from his partners' heated gazes to glance around the room and was thrown off guard when he saw Ophelia and Diana sitting together.

"Oh, I was under the impression this was strictly a staff meeting." He smiled at his ex-fiancée. "Not that I'm complaining."

"Actually, I am here on business." Ophelia smiled. "Diana and I have started our own management team and T&B have expressed interest in signing one of our artists."

Jonas's brows crashed together. "Have we now?" His eyes darted to his partners. "I don't think so."

"Excuse you?" Marcel blinked.

"What do you mean?" Ophelia asked in alarm.

Jonas laughed. "C'mon. I can't be the only one in the room thinking it." He looked again and caught a few amused faces before they thought to hide it. "Are your artists being signed for talent or because you're married to the owners of a record label?"

"Hinton," Marcel barked. "You're out of line."

"Am I?" he asked innocently. "I have an equal investment here. I have every right to question the validity of our artists, i.e. are they talented or just well connected?"

Ophelia's face darkened in anger. "You can't just come in here—"

"Oh, but I can." He smiled serenely and enjoyed, perhaps a bit too much, successfully getting under her skin.

Ophelia and Diana looked to their husbands while the room's tension thickened.

"This meeting is adjourned," Marcel announced, his jawline as hard as Stone Mountain.

The announcement was like a starter pistol shot

into the air, judging by the way the staff members bolted out of their chairs and raced from the room.

"Well," Jonas said, leaning back in his seat. "I hope it wasn't something I said."

Solomon leaned his elbows against the conference table and dropped his head into the palms of his hands. "One…two…three—"

"What the hell is he doing?" Jonas asked.

Marcel stood from his chair. "I'd say that he's trying not to kill you."

"Or at least letting me have the honors," Ophelia said, climbing out of her chair, as well. "How dare you embarrass me like that in front of the staff? You have no idea how hard and long Diana and I have been working with SisterSol."

"Good Lord." Jonas frowned. "Is that their name? What are they—a seventies retro band?"

"Those girls *earned* their record deal," Diana hissed. "How dare you suggest otherwise?"

Jonas tossed up his hands. "Whoa. Whoa. I'm sensing some hostility here."

"Damn right you are," Ophelia shouted. "You are supposed to be a silent partner. Do I need to get you a dictionary so you can look up the word *silent?*"

He shrugged. "I changed my mind."

"You have no experience in this industry. You're in completely over your head."

"Me? The last time I checked you were in the medical field. You mean to tell me after twenty months married to a music executive you're qualified to manage artists?" He looked to Diana. "Weren't you just a secretary before you married Marcel?"

"Enough," Solomon barked; his counting did little to calm him down. "We're going to have to have some ground rules around here. You're taking this revenge crap too far and I'd rather close the damn doors before I let you come in here and destroy everything we've built."

"Close the doors, eh? Don't tease me." Jonas stood. "I want to see this SisterSol group perform before I agree to any kind of record deal."

"Before you agree?"

"If they are as talented as you claim, then what's the big deal?" He headed toward the door. "If they're not, you'll have to shop them to another label."

"Asshole!" Ophelia snapped.

Jonas opened the conference-room door. "You know, I've been told that a lot lately."

"How did it go?" Michelle asked when Jonas returned.

"About as well as you can expect," he said.

"Well, at least you made it back without a busted lip. I'd say that's an improvement."

Jonas laughed. "I was thinking the same thing on my way over." He winked as he headed to his private office.

"You have a visitor waiting, by the way."

"Oh? Female or male?" he asked before he opened the door.

"Female—as usual," she said, shaking her head. "Lock the door, if you're going to be doing something I shouldn't know about."

"Will do...or you could knock."

"Actually, I'm about to go to lunch." She grabbed her purse. "Your next appointment isn't until three."

"Got it. Thanks."

Jonas opened his office door, hoping to see Toni, but was thrown off guard to see his attorney, Patsy, looking up from a stack of paperwork.

"Ah, there you are." She glanced at her watch and then stood with a smile. "You're going to love me, baby."

"Oh?" He closed his office door behind him. "I take it you have good news for me?"

"Great news." Patsy beamed. "You were right not to settle this claim with Ms. Gibson. This is not the first time she has sued an employer for sexual harassment nor is it the second or third time."

"You're kidding me."

"I don't kid about things like that."

Jonas's head snapped up.

"What?"

"Oh." He waved it off. "Nothing. Someone else I know says that a lot." His thoughts wandered as he walked over to his desk.

"Well?" Patsy asked. "Aren't you pleased?"

Jonas jolted from the memory of Toni's long legs and seductive curves. "I'm sorry. What?"

Patsy folded her arms with an amused smirk. "You're not thinking about business."

He almost denied the accusation, but he knew better than to try and pull the wool over Patsy's eyes. "You caught me. Sorry."

"That's all right." She glided saucily behind the desk. "We were both probably thinking about the same thing." She eased down onto his lap and wrapped her arms around his neck. "What do you say we go out for drinks and then do a little celebrating tonight—either your place or mine?"

Jonas chuckled under his breath while he thought about a tactful way out of the proposition. "I would, but, um…I sort of have plans," he lied.

"Cancel them," Patsy said, leaning in and stealing a kiss.

Jonas wrapped his arms around her waist. Maybe this was what he needed to get his mind off Toni's dark skin and sinful body. He deepened the kiss and Patsy moaned softly.

"So what do you say?" she asked, pulling back. "Is it a date?"

I ain't missing you at all…

Chapter 18

"I've missed you so much," Brian said, stretching his hands across the table. "Why haven't you called me?"

Toni smiled but her gaze remained locked on the ice cubes floating in her glass. "Well, I've been busy—trying to get my own practice up and running. It's a lot of work."

Brian's smile broadened across his handsome features and caused an old memory to rise to the surface.

"We were great together once," he whispered.

When he squeezed her hands, she pulled them back and rested them in her lap.

Brian heaved a dramatic sigh and eased back into

his chair. "What's wrong? You're not behaving like yourself this evening."

Toni brightened her smile though the effort nearly killed her. "Nothing," she lied.

Brian didn't pretend to believe her. "What's his name?"

Her heart squeezed and the smile vanished. "I'm sorry, Brian, but maybe I should go home."

His eyes glossed with restrained tears, but then his pride kicked into gear and within a blink they were gone. "You know...I still love you."

Toni nodded sadly. "Yeah. I know."

The club's music and low hum of chatter and laughter filled the silence between them. Toni went back to sipping her Coke and watching him nurse a glass of ginger ale. Years ago, she would have never dreamed such awkwardness would exist between them—but that was before she was introduced to his demons.

"I've been sober for eight months."

"And I'm happy for you. Truly, I am...but I can't do it. I can't go back." She sucked in a breath and could feel the pain of her childhood creep back into her heart. A childhood she had tried desperately to forget. Nothing this man could say would get her to travel down the same rough road as her mother.

Toni lost count of the number of black eyes, broken arms, ribs and busted lips her mother sustained all in the name of love. When Rosalind Wright finally summoned enough courage to leave, her husband decided that if he couldn't have her then no man would.

On the morning of Toni's fifteenth birthday, a drunken Anthony Wright tracked his wife and daughter down at an Atlanta women's shelter. When Rosalind spotted her husband in the parking lot, she'd convinced Toni to leave her side and run. Just when Toni had made it inside the building and shouted for help, she heard a gunshot. Toni jumped, pivoted toward glass doors. Her mother lay sprawled on the black asphalt. She glanced up at her father just as he stuffed the gun into his mouth and pulled the trigger.

That day changed her life forever.

"I had hoped that one day we would get—"

"You said you had some business you wanted to discuss with me?" she asked, hoping to successfully change the subject.

"Yes, but I was hoping we could—"

"Brian," she said firmly. "It's over. There is no future for us. You have to get that through your head."

A vein twitched against Brian's left temple—a sign she recognized from her father when he was close to exploding.

Toni squared her shoulders, prepared for anything—even in this crowded place. "I didn't come here to play games, Brian. Do you have business you want to discuss with me or not?"

Jonas arrived at Club Secrets with Patsy clinging and smiling on his arm. He dropped his name to the bodyguard at the velvet rope and was ushered past the long line and then up to the VIP section on the top floor. No sooner had he and Patsy taken their seats, did Jonas's gaze zoom to a table downstairs near the dance floor.

The woman's long crossed legs and smooth ebony shoulders caused the blood in his body to heat. What was it about Toni Wright that got under his skin? Why couldn't he stop thinking about her?

"Jonas?" Patsy touched his arm and captured his attention.

"I'm sorry. What?" He looked at her and saw a waitress standing at their table.

"I asked if you wanted to order a bottle of champagne?"

"Sure." He waved. "Whatever you want." He returned his gaze to Toni's table and for the first time, he noticed the man sitting with her.

Brian Olson.

Jonas clenched his jaw and flexed his hand into a tight fist. What the hell were they doing here together? Agitated, he shifted in his chair and continued to watch the couple closely. After a few minutes of reading the couple's body language, Jonas's jealousy waned and his curiosity grew.

Leaning forward, he tried to get a better view of Toni's face. Her straight shoulders, her firm profile—everything screamed that she was uncomfortable being there.

"You know," Patsy said, standing from her chair to ease into his lap. "It's considered impolite to ignore your date."

With his view of Toni blocked, Jonas heaved an

impatient sigh, but collected himself in time to ease on a smile. "You're right."

"Of course I'm right." She fingered his open collar as she leaned against his chest. "Gosh, I can't believe how long it's been," she whispered in his ear. "When I get you back to my place, I'm going to give you a night you'll never forget."

"Sure, baby. It will be great." Jonas swiveled his chair to the right so he could recapture his view of Toni and Brian.

"Your champagne, sir." The waitress returned to their table with their requested bottle chilling in a silver bucket of ice.

"Well, I see you finally made it."

Jonas sighed at yet another interruption. Turning, he glanced up to see a glowering Solomon standing near his table. Unable to stop himself, Jonas laughed. "Jesus, man. Smile. I'm beginning to think marriage doesn't agree with you."

Without waiting for an invitation, Solomon took a seat. "Don't worry about my marriage. It's solid."

Jonas shrugged. "I guess I'll have to take your word for it."

Patsy shifted on his lap. "You know, I think I'm going to just visit the ladies' room while you two talk."

The men ignored the announcement and Patsy hopped out of Jonas's lap with a dramatic roll of her eyes. "Try not to miss me."

Jonas stole a quick glance to Toni's table and relaxed when he saw she was still there.

"What will it take to buy you out?" Solomon asked with menace.

Jonas coolly quirked a brow. "Don't tell me I've worn out my welcome."

"Do you really need me to tell you that?"

Smiling, Jonas leaned back in his chair. "I'm not interested in selling. I have a feeling you boys are going to make me a lot of money."

The house lights blinked a few times and the club's volume dimmed considerably. In the next second, Ophelia took the stage in a beautiful aqua blue dress that reminded Jonas of the blue diamond he'd bought her as an engagement ring.

"I always thought she looked good in blue," he whispered.

Solomon promptly stood up from the table and left.

Jonas snickered behind his back. "Geesh. Can't pay some people a compliment nowadays." He reached over for the bottle of champagne and then glanced down at Toni's table.

She and Brian were gone.

Jonas's heart quickened as he bolted to his feet. Where did she go? Did she and her ex leave together? And if so, where are they going now?

An unbidden image of Toni sighing and moaning beneath the pencil-pushing geek had him rushing from the VIP area and navigating through a throng of people.

"Welcome to the stage: SisterSol," Ophelia announced, and the crowd responded with thunderous applause.

Jonas reached the door, pulled the bouncer aside and gave a brief description of Toni.

"Yeah. I saw her," the beefy man admitted. "She and some dude just left about a minute ago."

"Did they leave in the same car?" he demanded with his hands balling at his sides.

"Sorry. I can't help you out on that. I didn't notice."

Jonas muffled a curse and then slipped the man a bill. "My car."

The bouncer peeked at the hundred dollar bill. "Yes, sir." He rushed toward the valet and a few minutes later, Jonas was in his car and peeling away from the club.

A lone voice in the back of his head tried to calm him, but Jonas's raging emotions silenced it. At the moment, he didn't want anything to do with reason. He didn't want to hear about how he had no right to be jealous or had any say in who Toni saw, talked to or even slept with. He just knew that Brian Olson needed to keep his grubby paws off his…what?

Jonas shook his head—not wanting to get mired down with labels or lack of labels. He just knew that he was going to punch Brian's lights out if he was at Toni's. Screeching through Toni's subdivision, Jonas whipped his Mercedes up the circular drive and braked in front of the front door.

Incensed, he had no memory of actually getting out of the car or even bounding up the stairs. However, he was aware of pounding the door and determined to knock it off its hinges, if need be. "Open up, Toni! I know you're in there!"

Chapter 19

"**W**ho is it?" Toni's agitated voice roared from the other side.

"Me! Open up!" He continued to bang while the locks disengaged.

The door finally swooshed open and an angry Toni, wrapped in a silk, champagne-colored robe—and looking too damn sexy for her own good—glared back up at him. "What in the hell do you think you're doing?"

Jonas ignored the question and Bogarted his way into the house.

"Hey!" She slammed the door in his wake.

Still a man on a mission, Jonas searched the

kitchen, the living room, the dining room and then raced up the stairs.

"Jonas Hinton, you get back down here," she demanded, stomping her foot. When he continued to ignore her, she sprinted up the staircase mad enough to chew a handful of iron nails.

She found the deranged man in her bedroom, snatching open her walk-in closet and bolting inside like he was a member of the SWAT team.

"There's no one here," he said, his face twisted into a confused frown.

Toni crossed her arms and leaned against her bedroom's door frame. "Are we not counting the crazy nut job that just tore through my house looking for his imaginary friends?"

Jonas blinked and made another glance into the manless closet.

"There's still no one there," she said, her anger radiating in waves.

A few seconds of awkward silence lapsed between them before Jonas's lips sloped and his cheeks dimpled.

"Don't even think you can charm your way out of this," she warned.

Finally, he tossed up his hands. "Okay, okay. I might have been a little out of line."

Toni arched a singular brow. "Might?"

Straightening his shoulders, he strolled across the room, still relying on his charm to help him out of this mess. "I saw you tonight at Club Secrets…with your ex—Brian Olson."

Her gaze dropped to the floor and Jonas swore he sighted a sliver of emotion that he was curious and determined to get to the bottom of. "I apologize," he offered. "I saw you two together, I jumped to conclusions and I raced over here to…to…"

Hell, he hadn't thought this part through.

"You raced over here to what?" she asked. This time both of her brows crawled upward.

"To…make sure…that you didn't do something you might regret."

"What? Like sleep with Brian?"

The mere thought and the casual way she said it, stirred his jealousy anew. "Something like that."

"And you think I'd regret that?"

"Well, sex with an ex can usually lead to problems." Never mind that was exactly what he had planned for the evening. *Damn. He'd forgotten about Patsy.*

"Is that right?" she asked, still leaning casually against the door frame. "And who, pray tell, was the beautiful woman propped on your lap this evening?"

For the second time in five minutes, Toni had verbally fenced him into a corner.

"A friend," he barked, and coughed at the same time.

Toni's dark eyes flashed. "Do I look like I was born yesterday?"

Despite Jonas's collar buttons being open, he swore the damn thing was clenched tight across his Adam's apple. "No, um." He cleared his throat. "I think we've already established that you were born quite a few years before me."

Wrong choice of words.

"Are you deliberately trying to piss me off or is this something that just comes naturally for you?"

This time, he dropped his gaze. "No. I'm just trying my best not to admit that I…was jealous when I saw you tonight." His heart muscles squeezed so tight that for an insane two seconds he thought he was experiencing a heart attack.

While silence roared like a freight train between them, Jonas cursed himself for admitting that god-awful truth. So much for his plan to emotionally detach—to not be vulnerable—to not get hurt. The train appeared to roar on for forever and Jonas simply grew tired of waiting for her to say something.

"I better go." He moved to step past her in the doorway.

Toni unfolded her arms and caught him by the hand. "I was jealous, too."

Jonas froze and then slowly shifted his gaze back to her upturned face. The anger was gone and she looked soft and approachable—and still sexy as hell.

"When I saw you in the VIP room tonight," she whispered. "I was out of my chair so fast, I think I made Brian's head spin." She smiled.

"That's not so bad. I left my date powdering her nose in the ladies' room when I noticed you were gone. I'm willing to bet money she's pretty pissed off about now."

Toni laughed.

Jonas relaxed despite the warning bell sounding

off in his head and the growing hard-on throbbing against his pants leg. Her hands still held his and he caressed her long fingers.

"So what do we do now?" she asked, pressing up against him. "You want to run back to the club for your date or…" Her head tilted toward the cherry-wood sleigh bed.

His eyes followed her direction while a smile carved onto his lips.

"I have to warn you though," she added. "If you walk out this door, I'll probably shoot you."

Jonas released her hand only to slide his arms around her curved waist. "Wild horses couldn't drag me out of this bedroom." He leaned forward, anxious to taste her lips again and then moaned in pleasure when he found them sweeter than the last time.

Though she stood a half foot shorter than him, Jonas nonetheless felt overwhelmed by her soft curves and heavenly fragrance. When she moaned and twined her hands behind his neck, he deepened the kiss and scooped her up into his arms.

Tipping her back onto the pillows, Jonas simply crawled on top and continued to overindulge on her heady kisses.

Toni pulled at the buttons on his shirt and felt them pop off one at a time. When the last one pinged across the room, she peeled the fine material off his broad shoulders and roamed her hands across the wide span of his back. After her fingertips assessed every inch of him, she couldn't help but sigh with the results of their exploration.

Jonas came alive when Toni's hands tugged at his pants waistline. So much so that he was already grinding his throbbing sex against her thin silk robe and loving the way that she was grinding back.

He smiled against her lips. How refreshing it was to be entangled with a woman who knew what she wanted and how to get it—and yet there was nothing selfish about her lovemaking. She made sure to give as much pleasure as she took. Toni fed his starving body and still had a way of making him beg for more.

Who wouldn't like that in a woman?

Toni rolled Jonas over and saddled up on top. Her gaze latched on to his as she sucked in her bottom lip and teased him mercilessly by untying her robe's belt at a snail's pace.

When she'd finally slid the thin sash from around her waist and her robe parted down the center, Jonas wrenched his gaze from her heavy stare and dipped it down her body until it landed on her V of black curls.

Lord have mercy.

"Miss me?" she questioned softly.

Jonas bobbed his head and when she shed the robe from her shoulders, his mouth watered and he repeatedly licked his lips.

A laugh tumbled from her lips, teasing and mocking him; but he was so delirious with lust, he didn't give a damn. His greedy hands cupped her full breasts, his fingers and thumbs gently rotated her perked nipples until she gasped and squirmed with pleasure.

Two could play this game.

"Do you like that?" he asked, sitting straight up. When she stalled to answer, his fingers tightened on her nipples. "Hmm?"

"Y-yes," she panted.

He smiled and planted a trail of kisses along her collarbone and then blazed a new trail through the valley between her breasts. Lord, she smelled good.

"Let me finish helping you out of these pants," she suggested.

Nodding, he released her breasts and allowed her to push him back down onto the bed's pillows. He watched her through the mesh of his curly eyelashes while she crawled backward and tugged his pants and boxers down. His swollen sex sprang ramrod-straight into the air the moment the material glided off his hips and he didn't miss the glow of pleasure in her eyes.

When he was at last stripped nude, Toni perfected her catlike crawl back up his body and stopped when she'd reached his towering erection.

Curious about what she would do next, Jonas folded his arms behind his head and continued to watch her. Apparently, Toni wasn't finished teasing him. Her gaze found his through his curtain of lashes as she eased her head down before his throbbing cock.

Her warm breath drifting across his taut flesh was enough to do him in, but he kept his jaw set in re-straint. Yet after a few seconds of this unusual stand-off, his hips lifted on their own and tried to nudge his quivering sex against her lips.

Another sly smile slid across her full lips. "Is there something you want?" she asked.

Jonas didn't know when it had started, but he was suddenly aware his breathing was reduced to short puffs while his heart raced as if he'd just finished hiking up Mount Everest.

"Hmm?" she asked, and then slowly slid her tongue up his shaft once like it was her favorite lollipop.

He nodded and then nudged his cock against her mouth again.

She gave it another long lick.

Another nudge.

Another lick.

On the fourth lick, he was damn near ready to explode. Now how in the hell had she managed that? Her eyes narrowed at him as if suspecting his eruption and she gave him a disapproving shake of her head. "I don't think so, baby."

She cat-crawled the rest of the way up his body and then stopped when her knees cradled the sides of his head on the pillow.

Jonas gladly lifted his head and plunged his tongue deep into her pink cave. When she quivered in response, he lifted his arms and locked them around her hips. The power ball was back in his court and he was determined to hold on to it for as long as possible.

His tongue dived, twirled and pulsed inside of her. The room filled with the sound of her sighs, gasps and whimpers. Her orgasm, no doubt, hit with an

Olympic time and her knees bucked as she tried to crawl away.

However, Jonas felt the need to teach her a lesson and kept his arms locked around her hips and his tongue lapping at her flowing juices until another orgasm wrenched a scream from her hoarse throat.

Satisfied, he released her and she slumped over to the other side of the bed, panting as though she'd narrowly escaped his wild feasting with her life.

Jonas grabbed his pants from the floor and retrieved a condom from his wallet. Energized and emboldened by his short-lived dominance, he coaxed her legs and planted himself between. To his surprise, his hands trembled as he slid the latex over his straining flesh. He was desperate to get inside of her.

Still feeling loose-limbed and languid after her two incredible orgasms, a lazy smile slithered onto Toni's face as she watched Jonas's eyes glaze with unfettered passion. Her gaze drank in his gloriously nude body while she allowed him to toss her legs over his shoulders. When she felt his heavy shaft against her vaginal lips, she sucked in a breath in preparation of his body's invasions—but it wasn't enough.

He glided into her with one swift thrust and robbed them both of their very breath. He started off with long, measured strokes while rolling his eyes and sucking air through his teeth but after a long while, his pace quickened and the room's temperature rose to sweltering.

Dizzy and mumbling incoherently, Toni spiraled into sensory overload. Their heated flesh burned against each other while she made a feral wish that this night could last forever. Another orgasm rose to the surface as their rhythm turned frantic.

Her body jerked, contracting around his shaft, once, twice, and then another cry tore from her throat as a dazzling orgasm erupted within.

Jonas dove deeper, growling and praying at the same time. A storm of emotions rumbled and clashed within him. God, how he loved her body—loved what it could do and how it made him feel. Finally, their body's friction ignited something within and transformed his growls into a lion roar. He flinched, jerked and, at last, exploded inside of her.

When the last of his orgasm drained into her, he slumped forward and rested his head on the crook of her neck. "Oh, Toni. What have you done to me?"

Chapter 20

"How dare you leave me stranded at that club?" Patsy roared, storming into his office.

Jonas clamped his mouth shut and took his punishment because to offer an explanation would just land him into deeper hot water.

"How could you do that to me?" the incensed attorney raged. "I only had my ID and a tube of lipstick on me. Care to know how I made it home?"

"Patsy, I apologize. Something urgent came up," he regretfully lied.

"Urgent my ass. The bouncer told me you ran out of there looking for some woman. Most likely the one you kept staring at when you were supposed to be paying attention to me!"

Damn. Why didn't he keep his mouth shut?

An hour later, when he walked through the doors of T&B Entertainment, Ophelia opened a second can of whoop-ass.

"How dare you walk out the minute my girls take the stage? Their sole reason for performing was for you!"

Damn. He'd forgotten about SisterSol.

"Are you getting some kind of cheap thrill having everyone jump through hoops for you?"

"Sorry, something urgent came up."

"Urgent my ass! The bouncer told us you ran out of there looking for some woman."

"Probably that same woman I caught you staring at up in VIP," Solomon grunted.

Jonas swore under his breath. Apparently a hundred-dollar tip didn't buy silence nowadays. He chuckled to himself, but his amusement sent the wrong message to his business partners.

"I'm so glad wasting our time amuses you," Marcel said, bitingly.

Jonas tried to look contrite, but it was difficult since he couldn't stop the glorious images of Toni from streaming through his mind. The woman was thoroughly intoxicating to the point he found it difficult to stick to his plan: sex only.

The fact of the matter was: he wasn't ready to cast her aside. He would…eventually; but for right now, he wanted to get to know her better.

What was her story? What made her tick? And why in the hell hadn't someone snatched her off the market?

The last question caused laughter to rumble inside his chest. Toni Wright loved men and her independence too much. He imagined a man would have to hog-tie Toni and drag her to the altar.

He laughed again.

"Are you high, drunk or have you finally lost what few marbles you had left?" Marcel questioned.

Jonas cleared his throat and glanced around the table. All eyes were on him. "Fine. Fine. We'll sign the group," he said, caving. After all, it wouldn't hurt for him to give in a little. He glanced down at his watch and pushed away from the conference table. "I better go. I have somewhere I need to be."

Marcel and Solomon also glanced at their watches.

"But we're in the middle of a meeting."

"Well, I'm sure you two can carry on without me," he said, standing and then strolling toward the door. "Michelle can get me on my mobile if you need anything." He breezed out of the conference room, slamming the door behind him.

Marcel and Solomon's gazes zoomed to each other.

"We've got to do something about him," Solomon said. "And soon."

Toni couldn't stop smiling and feeling like a silly schoolgirl. Each time she thought about how Jonas worked her body, she experienced an orgasmic thrill that had her slumping back in her chair and craving a cigarette.

And she didn't even smoke.

After a few hours of this, the evitable question: how long would this last—surfaced in her mind.

How long did she *want* it to last? For months, she'd wanted him, now she had him—twice—and she was in that awkward phase when she estimated or counted down when it was time to move on.

If she wanted to move on.

"If," she repeatedly whispered up to the ceiling.

The last time she came across this crossroad was with Brian. She chose to stick around and that had turned into a colossal mistake. Sooner or later, men became too possessive, too clingy.

She couldn't breathe in clingy relationships.

There was no mistake about it: that danger lurked in Jonas's eyes. Just look at how he'd stormed over to her place, searching for another man—as if he had the right.

For the first time that morning, Toni's smile waned. She refused to belong to any man. *Love is a woman's greatest downfall.*

Anna, Toni's new secretary, buzzed into her office. "Ms. Wright, there's a Brian Olson here to see you."

Toni groaned and wondered why she didn't rent out an office with a back door.

"Ms. Wright?"

"Yes, yes." She sighed and glanced at her watch. "Send him in." Toni straightened in her chair.

Seconds later, Brian entered her small office,

wearing a wide smile and clutching an obviously heavy briefcase.

"Morning, Brian," she greeted in her best cheerful voice. "What brings you by this morning?"

His awkward laugh bounced off the office's thin walls before he took his seat. "Are you kidding me? You ran out of the club so fast the other night we never got around to discussing business."

"Oh? I thought you used business as a ruse to get me there."

He released another laugh and she noticed that there was something wrong with his body language. Tension was in his shoulders, eyes and facial features. "I thought I'd said something wrong and, uh, decided to swing by your place and—"

"But you don't know where I live," she said, her hackles starting to rise.

"Actually, I, uh, sort of Googled you."

The goddamn World Wide Web.

"You showed up at my place and…"

His eyes snapped to hers. "You had company."

The energy shifted in the room, bolting Toni to her feet. "You need to leave."

Brian didn't move. Instead, he shook his head while a crooked smile played across his face. "You really don't waste time, do you?"

"Brian, we'd agreed it was over."

He glared, his eyes darkening within seconds. "What kind of game are you playing by sleeping with one of the partners your practice is suing." Finally, he set his briefcase on the floor and stood from his chair. "I may be mistaken, but I think something like this would fall under 'conflict of interest.' What do you think?"

"I think you're out of line."

"I think you're nothing but a whore."

Toni stomped her foot. "Get out!"

Again, Brian ignored the order and bolted around her office desk to wrench hold of her arms.

Toni screamed and her office door burst open.

She blinked for several seconds before she believed her own eyes. Jonas had Brian smashed up against a wall with his hands twisted behind his back.

"What the hell do you think you're doing, man?" Jonas roared.

Brian tried to speak, but Jonas rammed the nervous attorney's head back into the wall.

"I have a better idea. How about you apologize to the lady?"

Brian's heated gaze seared Toni and she found herself plopping back down into her seat.

"I can't hear you," Jonas sneered, and rammed the man's head back into the wall.

"I-I'm s-sorry."

Another ram.

"I said I—I'm sorry."

Jonas glanced at her now. It took a moment before she looked at him and when she did, he was disturbed by the shock and horror written in her face. "Toni?" he said softly.

Tears rose to her eyes, surprising the hell out of

him and touching a tender spot in his heart. "What do you want to do? Call the police?"

"What? Wait," Brian protested. "There's no reason to call the police."

Jonas rammed the man's head again.

"Toni?"

Blinking out of her stupor, Toni shook her head. After all, what had he really done—grabbed her arm? She was suddenly embarrassed by her reaction. "No. Just…let him go."

Jonas twisted the man's arms.

"Aagh!" Brian roared.

"Are you sure?" Jonas asked.

"Yes, let him go," she shouted, equally irritated at Jonas. Was he trying to impress her with his brute strength? It was just like a man to think that was the only way to settle a dispute.

Jonas released Brian and then watched the man quickly slink away to grab his briefcase. "We'll talk later," he said to Toni.

"I don't think so."

Brian started to say something else, but Jonas cut him off. "All right. That's enough. You heard the lady."

Brian bolted out of the office.

Anna, who stood wide-eyed at the door, jumped out of Brian's way when he raced out and then looked to her boss. "Is there anything I can get you, Ms. Wright?"

"No. I'm fine. Thank you."

Anna hesitated, glanced at Jonas, and then finally left the doorway.

Jonas strolled over to the door and closed it to

give them some privacy. "Are you sure you're all right? You still look a bit shaken up."

And she was. Damn it. Even after several deep breaths, her body shook like the last fall leaf on the first day of winter. And for what? Her ex-boyfriend grabbed her?

"Toni?"

She swallowed. "I could've handled him," she said, unconvincingly. "I didn't need your help."

Jonas blinked and then held up his hands. "My bad. The rules for boyfriends must have changed in the last year or so."

The comment calmed her instantly. "Boyfriend?"

Hearing the word being tossed back at him, his smooth caramel coloring reddened. "Well, I guess I should ask whether the position is available."

Her smile was instant, but her answer wasn't. "Boyfriends," she said, finally feeling like herself again, "cause complications."

"So do girlfriends." He stalked his way to her desk. "By the way. You certainly know how to fill out a skirt."

Toni glanced down at her short black skirt. Her eyes narrowed as she looked back up. "Are you flirting with me?"

His gaze caressed her face. "I like flirting with you—even though it doesn't seem to have much effect." He stopped before her and leaned back against her desk. "Or does it?"

Toni smiled. "Are you trying to get inside of my head?"

Their eyes locked.

"I can think of something else I'd rather get into." His gaze lowered back to her long curvy legs. When he looked back into her eyes, she smiled. Standing up, her breasts brushed against his chest before she swept an arm across her desk, knocking everything to the floor.

Jonas chuckled but soon found his shoulders pinned to the dark mahogany surface. His smile disappeared when Toni, the tigress, climbed on top and pulled at his shirt until its buttons zinged across the room.

"You're costing me a fortune in shirts."

She quirked a brow. "You're complaining?"

He gave her a look of mock horror. "Never."

"I didn't think so." Her hands dove to his pants while her lips crashed against his.

Jonas moaned and plowed his large hands through her thick hair while he deepened the kiss. Still, the very talented Toni managed to slip down his pants while retrieving a condom from his back pocket.

After skillfully rolling on the latex, Toni simply hiked up her short skirt, pushed aside her blue thong and joined their bodies together.

Pulsing and bucking his hips beneath her, Jonas swore he'd died and gone to heaven. The things this woman could do, the way she continued to make him feel, pleased, as well as disturbed his peace of mind.

He wasn't so distracted not to notice there was something different in the way she used his body. She seemed more like a woman determined to prove something. Whether it was to him or herself, he wasn't sure.

Toni bounced, rocked and gyrated around his cock in a rhythm that had Jonas promising to give and do whatever she wanted. In his mind, nothing was off-limits: a mansion, cars, money—he didn't care. He would give it all to her as long as she didn't stop what she was doing.

Her body tightened—a telltale sign she was close to exploding. He sat up, pulled her body close and then swallowed her orgasmic cries as her body quaked and quivered all around him, setting off his own explosion.

Drained, they slumped against each other in a small cocoon of bliss. In this moment, Jonas knew without a doubt—he would never set Toni aside. He could never keep his emotions detached and he would do everything he could to keep her by his side.

Chapter 21

"Where are you taking me?" Toni asked, stealing a peek out of a small square window in Jonas's new private jet.

"It's a surprise." Jonas winked and then leaned back in the plane's plush leather chair. "Trust me. You'll love it."

Only one side of Toni's lips curled into a smile as she absently hand-ironed her short, black skirt against her legs. "How long are we going to be gone? You didn't let me go home to pack anything."

"Maybe I like you without clothes?"

Jonas watched as her brows climbed up her forehead and he realized he was becoming fond of the little habit. "Besides," he added. "You look like you need a vacation."

"I don't have time for a vacation." She sighed and stole another glance out of the window. "In case you forgot, I'm trying to get a new business off the ground."

"Ah, yes, by suing me."

"By suing your company."

"Same difference. And unfortunately you're wasting your time. Your client, Ms. Gibson had a personal relationship with William Bassett. It took me a moment, but I remember those two together when I attended Marcel and Diana's wedding. Ms. Gibson, was Mr. Bassett's date."

Toni shifted in her chair. "We have tapes."

"Audio?" he asked.

She nodded.

"We have video," he said with an impish smile. "I have to tell you—there are a few things on these tapes that even I wouldn't do. Well, maybe with the right woman." He jiggled his brows at her.

Lost for words, Toni blinked.

"Face it, Toni. You're being played. I hope you have other clients you can cash in on."

Stiffening in her chair, Toni's eyes narrowed. "I don't believe you."

"I take that as a no."

Carol, the jet's airline stewardess, approached. "Can I get you something to drink?"

"I'll just have a Diet Coke," Toni ordered, still reeling from Jonas's news.

"Make that two," Jonas said.

Toni's irritation melted into surprise.

"What?" he asked, catching her expression.

"Nothing," she covered with a smile and took a moment to reassess him.

Carol delivered their two chilled glasses of Diet Coke and then discreetly disappeared to the back of the plane.

"You know, it's way past time you told me more about yourself—and since we have a few hours to kill…"

"Hours?"

"At least," he shrugged.

Toni shook her head and returned her attention to the thick silvery clouds surrounding the plane. "There's not much to tell." Silence trailed her words and after a while Toni's curiosity caused her to chance a look in his direction.

"Why do you always do that?" he asked gently.

She swallowed. "Do what?"

"Evade the question."

"No, I don't," she lied.

Jonas cocked his head, slicing her with a cool, even gaze. "Is it because you don't trust me?"

Toni squirmed in her seat, tempted to snatch the life raft he'd tossed, but she couldn't force the lie to fall from her lips. Despite the short time they'd known each other, she did trust him. "No. That's not it."

"Then what?"

She shrugged again. "I just—I don't know. I don't like talking about myself. It doesn't do any good to get wrapped up in the past. You can't do anything about it."

Jonas frowned. "Our history is what makes us."

"No argument there," she mumbled.

"I'm curious about you," he pressed. "But I understand if you don't want to talk about it."

A second life raft. This time she was going to take it. "Thank you." To her surprise and horror, a small wave of tears stung the back of her eyes and threatened to breach the levies she had spent a lifetime building.

"How about…a foot massage?" Jonas set his drink aside and bent forward to grab one of her feet.

"That's okay." She instinctively tried to pull her foot from his grasp. "That's not necessary."

Jonas's grip remained firm. "No. Please allow me. I really would like for you to try and relax." He slipped off her beloved high-heeled pumps. "Ah, fresh as a daisy. I can't tell you how many points you would have lost if they had smelled like corn chips."

Toni laughed and then demanded his foot. "Let's see if you can pass the test."

Jonas gladly lifted his left foot and held a Cheshire-like smile as she slipped off his size fourteen shoes.

"Oh, good Lord." She tossed her head, fanned the air and then pretended to faint.

"Don't even play like that."

Toni erupted in laughter, but the moment his large hands began kneading the bottom of her foot, her head lolled back and she exhaled a heavenly sigh.

"Aw. You like that, do you?"

"Oh, God," she moaned. "Don't stop. Don't you ever stop."

Watching the myriad of emotions play across Toni's beautiful face was a potent aphrodisiac and Jonas again had to deal with his growing and throbbing hard-on. Things only grew worse from there.

Toni sighed, squirmed and arched her breasts high into the air until Jonas had to take a few seconds to *adjust* himself.

"Problem?" Toni asked, peeking through the mesh of her eyelashes.

He simply smiled. "Nothing I can't handle."

Toni slipped her foot out of his hands, lowering it to his lap and rubbing it against his stiff erection. "Now, this feels pretty damn good, too."

"Very funny." He reached for her foot again, but she evaded his grasp by digging her foot beneath his erection to play with his balls.

Jonas's brows popped to the center of his forehead. "Oh. You want to play?"

"I *always* want to play."

"Is that right?" Jonas took hold of her foot again and began working muscles she'd long forgot existed. Each movement and caress caused waves of pleasure to ripple up her legs and splash against her G-spot. Slowly, his hands left her foot only to climb past her ankle, calf and even the tender area behind her knee.

Toni was on the verge of an orgasm and the man hadn't even made it to her thigh. But then his lips took over and she suddenly found it difficult to keep oxygen in her lungs.

He hit a button on the side of her chair and she gasped when it instantly reclined. Her thoughts flew to the stewardess at the back of the plane.

"Jonas, maybe we shouldn't do this."

He looked up from the trail of kisses he planted on her thigh. "What? Are you scared?"

Toni's heart raced at the challenge in his eyes. "Not on your life."

Jonas's hands slipped behind her skirt and gingerly rolled her panties off her hips and down her legs. When his head lowered again, it rested between her V of curls. Upon the first stroke of his warm tongue, Toni's toned legs encircled his head and her long fingers roamed through his short hair.

He licked and sucked her body juices as though it was the elixir of life while Toni couldn't help but rotate her hips and try to feed him all that he could take. Given his skill and his tongue's powerful strokes, it wasn't long before Toni's orgasmic cries filled the cabin.

And still, he continued to feed.

She had barely caught her breath when her second orgasm detonated. This time she was sure the plane's captain heard her—and frankly, she didn't give a damn.

Minutes later, Toni completed her induction to the Mile-High Club by reclining Jonas back in his chair, climbing into his lap and riding him until he could spell her whole name both backward and forward.

Exhausted, neither knew who went to sleep first, but Jonas woke when the plane began its slow descent. He started to wake the sleeping bundle on his lap, but he was suddenly stuck by how beautiful and frail she looked.

The woman was definitely running from some terrible demons in her past. And he would be lying if he said that he wasn't hurt by her unwillingness to confide in him. Then again, maybe her elusiveness was another element that intrigued him.

Drawing a deep breath, he studied her for a few more seconds. Likely, such moments would be his only time to witness this incredible vulnerability. Did it make him a jerk for wanting to protect her from whatever she was trying to run away from?

Before making love to her in her office this afternoon, he thought all he wanted was to slide her into position as a playmate—a lover—a glorified booty call whenever the need arose and in return he wanted to take care of her. Money, cars—whatever. But now, his heart was demanding something else—something stronger, something long-lasting.

He closed his eyes and swore under his breath. How did he get himself back in this position?

He wasn't supposed to get attached.

He wasn't supposed to care.

He wasn't supposed to fall in love.

All three of those things would be easier to do if they weren't currently joined together and he couldn't feel her very heartbeat pulse all around him.

Jonas leaned forward and pressed a kiss against

her forehead. Maybe he could give love another try. See where the road takes him.

But could he recover if she broke his heart?

Alyssa's crush

Chapter 22

Alyssa was supposed to go to her room.

She also always had a hard time doing what she was told—especially now since the guests had started to arrive. Beautiful women draped on the arms of handsome men had her young, romantic mind churning and her body inching to be a part of the festivities.

Maybe she could.

The moment the possibility crossed her mind, her shoulders deflated when the promise she made her father floated back to haunt her.

"Cheer up, Alice. Things can't be all that bad."

Alyssa's head jerked up to see Quentin leaning against the oak door leading to the servants' quarters.

Her heart flip-flopped in her chest and when he flashed his dimpled cheeks, she nearly swooned on the spot. "What are you doing here?"

Q shrugged. "Well, if you don't want me here, I'm sure I can find a group of females who'd actually enjoy my company." He pushed away from the door and started to head back toward the wedding party. "I just thought you wanted to hear the rest of Jonas and Toni's story. Silly me."

"Wait." She raced over to him and grabbed him by the wrist. "I do."

When he turned to face her, she was suddenly stunned by her own behavior and released his hand while embarrassment scorched her entire body.

"Ah. So you are interested?"

She was much more interested in spending time with him.

He laughed. "What is it about women that make them love sappy love stories?"

Women? Did he consider her a woman now?

Alyssa straightened and even tried to thrust up her flat chest. Her effort wrangled another laugh from him. "Calm down." He tugged her fat pigtail. "Don't try to grow up so fast, sport. You have plenty of time to torture the opposite sex, Alice."

She smiled, enjoying their developing friendship. "It's Alyssa," she said meekly.

"What?"

"My name." She shrugged. "It's Alyssa—not Alice."

"Alyssa," he repeated; his eyes sparkled like diamonds. "I like it."

Another flash of his dimples and her knees nearly folded.

"Now, about this story." He leaned back against the door. "I can't tell you all of it, but if you tell me where you left off, I can tell you what I do know…."

Chapter 23

"Where are we?" Toni asked, peeking out of the window while trying to make herself presentable. The only problem was she couldn't make anything out other than a small runway surrounded by lush green trees.

"I told you," Jonas said, looking shamelessly delicious in his buttonless dress shirt and rumpled pants, "it's a surprise."

She hesitated—not out of mistrust—but because of overwhelming incredulity. It wasn't like handsome men whisked her away like this on a daily basis.

"C'mon," he added with a wink, and extended his arm. "You can trust me."

Smiling, she linked her arm through his and followed. The moment the cabin's door opened, a brilliant sun perched high above scattered cottony clouds nearly blinded Toni and she impulsively clutched Jonas's arm.

When her eyes adjusted beneath the shield of her free hand, she made a quick panoramic scan. Still, she could see nothing but a landscape of lush green trees and a beautiful cerulean sky.

But there was something else.

The air was different.

Just as her feet stepped off the last metal stair, a gust of wind whipped out of nowhere and caused her tousled mess of hair to start flapping around her face. It also caused her entire body to pimple against the cold.

"Are we by the ocean?"

Jonas just flashed her with his adorable dimples and turned his attention to two approaching Jeeps.

The moment the vehicles stopped, two ebony-rich colored men bounded out of one and raced to the side of the plane.

"That's not necessary," Jonas called to the men. "We didn't bring any luggage." He then turned toward an older gentleman with twinkling black eyes.

"It's been a long time, Mr. Hinton," the man said in a thick Caribbean accent. "Everything has been prepared as you've ordered. If there is no luggage I can take you to your chartered boat."

Toni blinked in further astonishment. "There's a boat ride, too?"

Another flash of dimples and Jonas approached the Jeep and opened the back door for her. "After you, my love."

Toni's stomach clenched at the casual endearment, but she painted on a smile and climbed up into the vehicle. Jonas jogged to the other side and climbed in. A few seconds later, they were off.

More wind streamed through Toni's hair and ruffled her clothing as if it was trying to take them off, but none of that mattered. At this moment in time, she was happy—positively giddy with excitement.

Where were they going?

What had Jonas planned?

Why had he called her "my love"?

She cast a look in his direction, momentarily surprised to find him staring. "What?" she shouted above the gusty wind.

Jonas continued on with his secretive smile and shook his head. "Nothing," he shouted back.

"Liar!"

That wrestled a laugh from him.

"C'mon. Give," she pressed.

Finally he shrugged and leaned closer. "You just look so beautiful when you're happy."

Touched, she smiled. "Well, what can I say? You definitely know how to sweep a girl off her feet."

His arm glided around her waist in silent possession and to his surprise, she tensed. He frowned, but then she relaxed again.

Minutes later, Jonas and Toni arrived at the Sapphire Marina and were escorted to a stunning wind racer yacht. Toni didn't think it was possible but more butterflies filled her stomach while Jonas greeted the boat's captain. After boarding and harnessing their life vests, they were off once again; this time, sailing through the tranquil blue sea.

Jonas had taken her to paradise.

But the best was yet to come.

"You have your own private island?" she asked incredulously as they approached a magnificent green vista.

"Actually, it belongs to my father," he responded with another squeeze to her waist. "He made most of his money in real estate."

"Pretty damn good real estate." She sighed.

"We think so." Jonas followed her gaze to his favorite hideaway.

They docked and then took another Jeep ride on the private island. Jonas finally escorted Toni into the verdant hillside Château Maria.

Toni tried to absorb the warmth of the carved teak-and-mahogany wood. Everywhere she looked there was polished granite, coral and marble tile. Whoever decorated the place obviously had an artistic eye for rich regal décor—a nice contrast against the secluded tropical forest outside.

Jonas gave her the grand tour through the winding terrace, railed wooden decks and even stone paths.

"This isn't a house. This is like a compound," she said after reaching the third floor of the grand château.

"Does that mean you like it?"

"What's not to like? This is paradise."

"I think so. Now that you're here."

Toni playfully narrowed her eyes. "Are you trying to get all mushy on me?"

He couldn't resist leaning in and delivering a quick peck to her upturned nose. "I might be." Another kiss. "Why don't you indulge me for the weekend?"

As was her habit, a lone eyebrow crept to the center of her forehead. "I just might do that."

In the master bedroom, Toni's eyes instantly went to the carved mahogany king-sized bed and her imagination took flight.

"All in due time, my love," Jonas promised. "All in due time." He headed over to the closet and pulled it opened. "All of these should fit you." He turned and faced her. "A size eight, right?"

Toni joined him at the closet and quickly sorted through the stunning selection of island clothing—the majority of them being scanty two-piece swimsuits.

"Since you have the body, you may as well show it off," he whispered.

"And pray tell what will you be wearing?"

"Well," he said, pulling her into his arms, "as little as possible."

The first thing Toni wanted to try out was the polished marble shower room. She quickly found out that such an endeavor was like showering beneath a waterfall and after a few adjustments she was quite content to spend the entire weekend in the shower. That was, of course, until an impatient Jonas joined her and showed her other things that could be enjoyed in a spacious shower room.

Many other things.

Once they were dry and quite satisfied, Jonas further surprised Toni by proving to be quite apt in the kitchen.

"You cook, too?" Toni asked, stealing a morsel from one of the serving bowls and then moaning in sheer pleasure when it melted against her taste buds. "Strike that. You're a chef."

Jonas chuckled and plopped another piece of his perfected sea bass into her mouth. "I had a great teacher. My parents' personal chef, Alfred, a lion of a man and an absolute genius in the kitchen, I learned a great deal from him."

"No doubt you shamelessly parade your cooking skills before all the women you've dated."

"Not all. Just one other."

Stunned, Toni blinked and then studied his face to see if he was pulling her leg. When she saw that he was serious, she decided to chance another question. "And how many women have you brought to this paradise island?"

Jonas met her gaze unblinkingly. "You're the first."

The impulse to call him a liar stayed on her tongue when she realized he was telling the truth.

"What? No snappy comeback?"

She shook her head, but continued to study him. "Why me?"

"I'll let you in on another little secret."

He smiled and pulled off another piece of fish and lifted it to her lips. "I like you."

* * *

Toni liked Jonas, as well—however, the electricity crackling between them hinted at something stronger.

And that scared the hell out of her.

However, Jonas gave her little time to reflect over her feelings. He was too busy making her laugh over his childhood stories and antics with his brothers. Jonas, the oldest, enjoyed his preteen years by being the head ringleader. He and his younger brothers had always had a thing for the *Godfather* movies and Jonas cast himself in the lead role.

He'd dole out childish orders like putting firecrackers in potpourri dishes, dyeing their mother's beloved toy poodle blue and even stuffing bananas in their father's car tailpipe à la *Beverly Hills Cop*.

Sterling may have been the middle child, but he was always the most serious of the three and he would always try to talk his brother out of issuing such dangerous orders that would guarantee spankings or thirty-day restrictions inside their rooms. In the end, he would carry out Jonas's orders and they would eventually get those spankings and restrictions.

Quentin was apparently born the clown and was the dominant skirt chaser. The brothers cast Q in the part of Fredo—since he was usually the leak or snitch in the group. This also meant he was beaten up by his brothers often. Then there was the prank that landed them the mother of all punishments.

"You staged a kidnapping?" Toni asked with incredulous laughter.

"We were mobsters," Jonas said, leaning over and refilling her wineglass. "Mobsters kidnapped people."

Tossing her head back against an easy chair, she laughed toward the night's twinkling stars. They had moved their private party down to the island's white-sanded beach. The sounds of the soft waves crashing against the shore, a crackling bonfire before them and the heady taste of Pinot Gris had her feeling more than mellow.

"Who did you kidnap?"

"Quentin."

"What? How did you kidnap a member of your own family?"

"Fredo needed to be taught a lesson. Of course, we didn't really count on my parents freaking and calling the FBI."

"See? I was always afraid that if I had kids they would be just as bad as you and your brothers."

An image of Toni with a pregnant belly flashed inside Jonas's head and caused his lips to curl into an instant smile. "Well, we turned out all right. We avoided a federal charge—since the agents cracked the case within two minutes of being on it."

Toni laughed and sipped her drink.

Jonas watched her—studied her while basking in the gentle sea breeze. "What about you?"

She stopped laughing but a smile lingered on her lips. "What about me?"

"C'mon. You can't tell me you were a perfect model princess who never got into trouble?"

Her smile slowly vanished. "No, I'm not going to tell you that."

His gaze dropped when he realized that he'd crashed into the same brick wall. Her past was clearly off-limits. After a long quiet moment, Jonas shifted his eyes back to their crackling fire.

"I don't have any brothers and sisters," she admitted softly. "And I certainly wasn't anyone's princess."

Jonas turned and gave her his full attention.

"I didn't pull pranks or...do a lot of childhood things."

He waited, sensing that she wanted to say more, but she never did. Unwilling to let the mood sour, Jonas bounded out of his chair, the firelight highlighting his well-muscled and toned body.

"How about a swim?" he asked.

Toni took her time appreciating his godlike form in swim trunks. "What makes you so sure I know how to swim?"

Stunned, he blinked and then laughed. "You're joking."

"Let me guess," she said playfully. "You grew up with a huge pool in your backyard."

Jonas walked over to her chair and offered his hand. "Come on. I'll teach you."

"Teach me? I'm forty—"

"Doesn't matter. I can teach you anything."

She hesitated, but a determined Jonas simply leaned down and scooped her into his arms. "What are you doing?" she squealed as he headed toward the water.

He laughed. "What do you think?"

"No. No. Put me down." She kicked her legs and tried to squirm her way out of his arms, but he wasn't having any of that.

Lucky for her, it was a full moon and it reflected off the clear water like a large mirror.

"Jonas, please. Please. Things live in this water."

"That's part of the beauty of it."

Before she could utter another protest, Jonas gently dipped her into the cold sea. Squealing, her arms tightened around his neck. "Don't let me go!"

"Don't worry," he said, his warm breath drifting across the shell of her ear. "I have you."

To her surprise, she relaxed, trusting him not to drown her and...something else. She glanced up into his eyes, completely taken by surprise by the soft tenderness glowing in them.

Something was happening between them. She could feel it in the marrow of her bones and in the fierce pounding in her heart.

True to his word, Jonas taught her how to remain afloat in the water, his hands casually gliding over her body, causing a different army of goose bumps to pimple her flesh.

"There you go. You're getting the hang of it," he encouraged, smiling.

Whether it was the truth or not she didn't know or care. Suddenly her body was infused with a new energy and it scared and excited her.

Jonas leaned back in the water and pulled her body so she floated on top of him. All the while, his gaze entrapped hers, pulling her toward something that she didn't know whether she was ready for or if she could handle it.

When she was finally able to pull her gaze from his, it was only for it to travel down to his lips. Next, she didn't know whether she kissed him or he kissed her; but she melted against him all the same and moaned so deep that it reverberated in her bones.

She had no recollection of how they made it from the sea back to shore, but she was keenly aware that she wasn't having sex with Jonas.

She was making love to him.

Chapter 24

"**Y**ou're alive!" Brooklyn declared when Toni opened her door. "Yeah, she's here," she then said into the Bluetooth latched on her ear. "Let me call you back." Without waiting for an answer, Brooklyn disconnected the call. "Where have you been? You had me worried."

Toni frowned and closed the door behind her friend. She had just returned home from her weekend excursion less than an hour ago and frankly she was still floating on cloud nine. "What are you doing here?"

Brooklyn turned on her heel and stabbed her with an incredulous look. "Isaiah and I came to visit his mother. I told you that two weeks ago on

the phone, remember? You said we should get together and go shopping."

Slapping a hand across her forehead, Toni realized she'd forgotten. "I'm so sorry, Brooklyn."

"Don't be sorry. Tell me where you were…and
why you're glowing."

Toni shrugged and pretended not to know what
her friend was talking about. "I just went out of town
for the weekend." She headed toward the kitchen.

"With?"

Toni removed a bottle of wine from the cabinet
and then proceeded to find two glasses.

"Hello?" Brooklyn waved a hand in front of her
friend's face. "Who did you go out of town with?"

"Who said I went with someone?"

Brooklyn laughed. "Why are you being so eva-
sive? I'm your girl. We tell each other everything."

She was right. Toni stopped buzzing around the
kitchen and turned to face her girlfriend. But what
could she say—that the impossible had happened?

"Just tell me you didn't hook back up with Brian.
I think I can take anything but that."

Toni laughed. "Then you can relax. Brian and I
are history."

"Good." Brooklyn straightened. "I liked him at
first but…" She didn't finish the sentence and she
didn't need to. Brooklyn studied her friend. "Well,
whoever it was, he must be awfully special."

Toni poured the wine and handed a glass to
Brooklyn.

"Can I at least get a name?"

"Jonas," she finally supplied. "Jonas Hinton." She marched out of the kitchen and entered the living room.

"Why does that name sound familiar?" Brooklyn asked, trailing her.

Toni settled on the couch and pretended to pick at a loose thread on her capris. She still didn't know what to say. She hadn't had much time alone to figure the whole thing out.

"Toni?" Brooklyn pressed, taking the spot next to her on the couch. "I've never seen you like this."

"I've never felt like this," she admitted. "And I definitely don't know what to do about it."

"Antoinette Wright, are you in love?"

"You're sleeping with the enemy?" Marcel thundered, bursting into Jonas's office.

"He *is* the enemy," Solomon corrected, storming into the room, as well.

Not surprisingly Brian Olson brought up the rear.

"Come in, gentlemen," Jonas said with an impatient sigh. "Make yourself at home."

"What is *really* going on here?" Marcel questioned, leaning over Jonas's desk. "You pop out of nowhere and buy a share of our company. At the same time we get hit with a frivolous lawsuit from Nora Gibson and lo and behold you're screwing her attorney?"

"I advised you once to watch your tone," Jonas warned. "You're talking about a woman I happen to care a great deal about."

"Really?" Solomon asked, startled.

"I think they're both in on it," Brian said, crossing his arms. "There's no such thing as coincidence."

Jonas sliced a lethal glare at the attorney. "I have a hard time believing Toni ever had anything to do with you." He took the man's measure and made sure Brian read his contempt.

Marcel and Solomon shared a befuddled look.

"I have to admit, I don't know what to make of all of this," Marcel said, pacing. "Are you legitimately in this business to make money or are you really set on revenge and trying to take us down?"

Jonas eased back into his chair, marveling at how he'd forgotten about his initial plans of revenge in such a short time. "The lawsuit also has my name on it. It doesn't make sense for me to be masterminding a petty lawsuit to get back at Solomon for stealing my fiancée."

"I didn't steal anything that belonged to you."

"Gentlemen. Gentlemen," Marcel cut in. "Let's stick to the matter at hand." He turned to face Jonas again. "We're prepared to buy you out. Name your price."

Jonas drew a deep breath as he cast his gaze about the room. When he'd bought Warner Music Group's shares in T&B Entertainment, he planned to be a constant pain in Solomon's side.

Misery loved company after all.

Funny thing was: he was no longer interested in revenge. He didn't care one iota about how happy or unhappy Solomon and Ophelia were. He was… over it.

A soft chuckle tumbled from his chest.

"What is so funny?" Solomon challenged, his irritation climbing to new heights.

"You know what, guys?" Jonas said, snapping out of his chair. "I think I will sell."

"Don't be ridiculous," Toni said, waving and laughing at her friend. "I'm not in love. I can't be."

Brooklyn laughed. "And why can't you be? You're still human, aren't you? You're still a woman." She reached over and pinched her friend's arm.

"Ouch."

"You appear to still have feelings so being in love is still a possibility."

Toni didn't care for the wry smile sloping her friend's face. "You're enjoying this, aren't you?"

"Damn right I am. I've been waiting for this moment for over twenty years." She kicked off her shoes and folded her legs beneath her. "So when do I get to meet this man? Maybe we can all go out on a double date before Isaiah and I head back to Texas."

"Slow your roll." Clinging to denial for all it was worth, Toni shook her head, trying to put the brakes on this whole thing before Brooklyn actually started planning a wedding. "It's not going to happen. Jonas and I are just having a good time. Nothing more. Nothing less."

Brooklyn's excitement plunged as she released a long sigh and rolled her eyes. "Why am I not surprised?"

Toni pressed her lips together in an effort not to ask Brooklyn what the flippant comment was supposed to mean. To do so would undoubtedly unleash an unwanted speech.

"You know," Brooklyn ventured with caution. "Not all men are going to be like your father."

So much for preventing a speech.

"I don't want to talk about this, Brooklyn."

"You never want to talk about it," she countered. "And that would be fine if I thought you've completely healed or have put the whole thing behind you but—"

"I *have* put the whole thing behind me," Toni thundered, bolting out of her seat and then pacing before the sofa. "I've gone through great pains to avoid the same mistakes my mother made and you know what? It's worked."

"A little too well, if you ask me."

Toni's brows crept upward.

"I know. I know. You didn't ask me." Brooklyn flittered a dismissive hand in the air. "Just like I didn't ask you to help me."

The two friends made eye contact while Brooklyn drew a deep breath.

"Look, Toni. You're my best friend. You've been there for me through two marriages and two children. It's only natural for me to want you to have the same type of happiness you helped me obtain."

"I *am* happy," Toni insisted. "Deliriously happy."

Brooklyn cocked her head.

"I mean…I come and go as I please. I don't have to answer to anyone. Nobody owns me and I don't own anybody. My life is perfect." Her voice quivered at the end, bringing attention to the lie.

Brooklyn remained silent.

Giving up the ghost, Toni drew a deep breath and slumped back onto the sofa. "I'm just saying that marriage isn't for everyone."

"But love is," her friend countered. "Look, Toni. I'm not saying you *need* to be married. You know me better than that. But to deny yourself love…well, that's another story entirely."

Toni was still shaking her head while her thoughts skipped down memory lane.

"I know the kind of pain love can bring."

"Your husbands never beat you."

"No. But there's domestic violence in my family—probably in everyone's family. And I'm not belittling what you went through—witnessing your father…but at least open your heart to the possibility of there being more out there than physical satisfaction."

That seemed to be happening to her whether she wanted it to or not. Jonas had already reached her heart in a way that no man had ever done before and she was ashamed to say that the whole experience frightened her.

"*Do* you love him?"

Toni choked, sputtered and choked some more.

Brooklyn crossed her arms. "Are you all right?"

"F-fine." She reached over and refilled her glass.

"Good. I'm still waiting for an answer."

Suddenly she was hit with a strong sense of déjà

vu. Four years ago, Toni was the one interrogating Brooklyn about her feelings for Isaiah. "You're enjoying this, aren't you?"

"Immensely."

Toni shook her head, her emotions still twisted in knots. She had almost given love a try before—of course, what she felt for Brian paled in comparison to how Jonas made her feel. "Life isn't fair."

"Who said it was?" Brooklyn again tossed Toni's words back at her with a smile. "My whole point is, you're right. Love can be scary and painful—but with the right person, it can be wonderful and exciting, with or without a ring." She draped an arm around her friend. "I just think it's time you stop running from it."

Toni managed a quivering smile; but in truth, she felt her friend was asking an awful lot from her. "I'll think about it," she assured her, though she was already sure she'd made up her mind on the issue.

Chapter 25

"It's not you. It's me," Toni said, clutching Jonas's hand across the white linen tabletop. Jonas's personal chef, Raul, had prepared a wonderful Mediterranean meal out on the condo's grand balcony while soft, classical music played through the outdoor speaker.

Jonas pulled his hand back as the candlelight flickered from the night's cool breeze. "What do you mean?"

Toni plastered on a smile, but she had a devil of a time meeting his eyes. "Look, we had some fun but…neither one of us are ready for anything more serious than that."

Jonas slowly eased back in his chair, trying to

pretend a bomb hadn't just exploded in his face. "Are you telling me this or are you asking me?" he questioned. He was just moments away from opening his heart and spilling his guts.

"Don't get me wrong. I had a wonderful time in the Virgin Islands. Certainly, it was one of the most romantic trips I've ever been on, but the truth of the matter is…I'm…"

She hesitated.

Jonas's brows dipped, sensing Toni wasn't exactly being truthful about her feelings. Was this just her way of trying to protect herself? Hope bloomed in his chest as he reached for her hand again.

She dodged his touch. "We had an agreement, remember?"

His features twisted in confusion. "What?"

"The ability to walk away."

Damn. He did say that…but that seemed so long ago and it certainly didn't reflect how he felt now. "Toni, a lot has happened between us since then. Feelings have changed."

"My feelings haven't," she managed to say casually through a firestorm of emotions. "I have too much going on in my life and—"

"Why are you doing this?" he asked. "Do you think things are going too fast? Do you want me to slow it down? We can slow things down." Slow was better than nothing.

"No. It's just…" She struggled to remember her rehearsed speech. She'd been giving this speech for over thirty years and suddenly she was having trouble getting the words out.

Maybe because she didn't really want to do this.

"Why don't you just be honest with me—with yourself?" he pressed. "How can you deny there's something…*magical* between us?"

"Magical?" She blinked. "C'mon now." She covered with a smile. "Don't get all mushy on me."

"Toni—"

"Look, you're a great guy and everything and someday you'll make—"

"Don't you dare say 'I'll make some lucky woman a wonderful husband,'" he hissed, and then slammed his fist down on the table. "Don't you dare!" Why in the hell was this happening to him again?

Toni jumped and then glanced at Jonas with frightened eyes. At seeing the anger and irritation lining the muscles of his face, anxiety clenched around her heart like a vise.

"I better go." She slid back her chair; but before she could rise from her seat, Jonas's hand whipped out and grabbed her wrist.

"No," he said, and then gentled his voice. "Please. Don't leave." He looked around at the table. "We haven't had dessert yet."

Frozen in her chair, Toni's gaze fell to his firm grip.

Jonas followed her eyes. "Sorry." Reluctantly, he released her. "Please. Stay."

His plea, along with his warm gaze, made it a real struggle to turn him down. How in the world did she ever think she could just keep things sexual with him? In retrospect, he'd gotten under her skin with very little effort. Was this how it felt to have a soul mate? Did she now believe in such things?

"I think I better skip dessert." She flashed an uneven smile. "Good night." She bolted out of her chair and raced from the balcony like a starlet from an old black-and-white movie. The rub was she knew that she was overreacting, but damn if she could help herself.

"Toni," Jonas called after her.

She didn't stop.

She refused to stop.

It wasn't because she was physically afraid of him, but afraid he could and would convince her to stay.

Not just for the night—but for a lifetime.

"Toni," he called again.

When her hand landed on the knob of the front door, Jonas's steel grip, once again, seized her small wrist a second before he spun her around.

"Let me go!" she screamed, trying to wrench her hand free.

"What the hell?" Stunned, Jonas released her and jumped back. "You were about to leave without your purse and coat."

Her burning face shifted from anger to embarrassment. However, her chest heaved from her sprint across the spacious condo.

"What the hell is going on with you?" Jonas said; things were starting to click in his head. "What is this really about? Why are you running from me?"

She drew a breath, ready to recite her rehearsed speech.

"And don't insult me by feeding me more of that crap you just gave me out on the terrace." He closed the sparse space between them. "I've seen you like this once before."

She clamped her mouth shut, momentarily thrown off guard.

"In your office," he continued. "With Olson." His narrowed gaze studied her. "Tell me I'm wrong."

Toni drew a few deep breaths, collected herself and tried to regain control of this situation. "I don't *do* long-term relationships," she admitted. "I'm no good at them."

Jonas folded his arms; after a while, he lifted his chin, satisfied that she had at least told him part of the truth. "You were afraid of me a minute ago," he said matter-of-factly. "Why?"

She hesitated.

"You thought I was going to hurt you," he added.

"No," she lied, and then tried to laugh it off.

Jonas didn't buy it and he grew angry with the conclusion his brain leaped to. "Who hurt you in the past?"

"No one," she lied again, and continued with her awkward laugh. What the hell was wrong with her? She usually had a better poker face than this.

The lies just continued to irritate Jonas. "Was it Olson? That weasel attorney?" His hands clenched into fists.

"No!"

"Then who?" Jonas thundered, slamming a fist against the door behind her.

The loud bang and sudden rattle caused Toni to yelp and jump. "I want to end this. Now."

Jonas shook his head. He couldn't possibly be going through this yet again. "Toni," he said, reaching for her.

Again, she sidestepped him and avoided his touch.

"Don't make this harder than it needs to be," she pleaded. "We haven't been together long. It's not like…"

"What?" he barked. "Like we *love* each other?" This time when he reached for her, she didn't turn him away. "What if I said I have fallen for you?"

Her gaze dropped to the incredible wide span of his chest. A knot of emotion lumped in her throat and rushed a river of tears to the back of her eyes.

Her gaze dropped and refused to lift again.

Jonas laughed. What else could he do? It was the second time he'd put his heart on the line and the second time a woman stomped all over it. "I can't believe that Q was right." A strange laugh bubbled in the back of his throat.

Toni eyed him warily as his laughter rumbled like a madman. "Right about what?"

"That when it comes to women, you keep your heart out of it. Evidently, I'm a slow learner." His eyes sparkled as if seeing her for the first time. "But *you* figured this stuff out a long time ago, didn't you?"

Toni tried to back away, but then realized she was already pressed up against the door.

"You never wanted my heart in all of this, did you?" he asked, removing all trace of humor from his voice.

"Jonas—"

"Answer the question," he hissed.

She closed her eyes and tried not to concentrate on how his warm breath heated her entire body and on how his bulging erection pressed against her pelvis.

"You've only wanted one thing from me, haven't you?"

"Jonas—"

"Haven't you?" He shifted ever so slightly to press his steel-like erection against her. He leaned forward and nipped at her ear. "Was I getting too serious for you? Hmm? Did I break a cardinal rule?"

When he drew her lower lobe between his teeth, her body trembled deliciously. But wait. She was supposed to be breaking things off.

"I can change it up, baby." He turned his head and found her lips. "Sex with no strings attached. Is that it? Is that all you want?"

She tried to answer, but the way he ground against her brought her dangerously close to an orgasm.

"What's the matter, baby?" he asked, his fingers already making quick work of the buttons on her blouse. "Are you afraid to play with fire?"

"Jonas," she panted. Whatever else she was going to say was cut off when his lips covered hers again. Seconds later, Jonas unzipped his pants, hiked her up against the wall, pushed the thin string of her thong aside and entered her with one smooth stroke.

To neither of their amazement, she was lush and more than ready for him. He reached down and gripped her satiny butt cheeks. She engulfed him to the hilt, her round bottom pressed against him and the door.

"Is this what you want, baby? Hmm?"

"N-no." *Yes.* Hell, she didn't know what the hell she wanted.

"No? You want me to stop?" His hips slowed to a torturous pace. "Say it and I'll stop."

"No," she muttered again.

"No stop or yes stop?"

"Don't. Stop." She bucked against him, silently urging him to pick up the pace.

Jonas was only too happy to oblige.

His smooth thrusts became quick hammerings and Toni had to wrap her hands around his shoulders in order to hang on for the ride. The door bucked and rattled behind her, but all she could think of was the glorious sensations building inside of her, dragging her closer to the brink of madness.

"C'mon, baby. You feel the fire, yet?" Jonas questioned. "Hmm?"

A small warning shot off in the back of Toni's head. There was something different in Jonas's tone—a dark edginess.

"I want you to get what *you* want. What *you* need," he hissed.

Hard as she tried, she really couldn't concentrate on his words because her body was too busy gloriously responding to his exquisite thrusts.

Hard.

Rough.

Deep.

Damn, she could barely breathe, let alone think. Her fingers dug into his flesh while he rammed her against the door.

Jonas watched his wildflower through budding angry tears. She was so beautiful. So passionate. So exciting. Why couldn't she be his and his alone?

"Oh, God!" Her nails sank deeper into his flesh.

He sucked in his pain and continued to thrust forward while she bucked fiercely against him. Her body clenched and quivered around him with her orgasmic release and he could feel a rush of her body's sweet juices around his cock—spurring his own wild, hot, pulsing release.

"Aargh!" he roared against her ear.

Her vaginal muscles continued to grip him tight.

With one last thrust, he shoved his entire length into her, roaring out as he emptied everything he had.

When it was all over, their harsh breathing and their desperate pants mingled together for a full minute. Finally, Jonas lowered her legs back down to the floor and then tucked his limp, sex-glazed organ back into his pants.

Without a word, he retrieved her purse and coat from the nearby closet, handed them to her and then opened the front door.

He was kicking her out.

"It's not you. It's me," he said evenly.

Toni sucked in a startled breath, cut a gaze to his stone, expressionless features and felt her heart shatter into a million pieces.

But wasn't this what she wanted?

If so, why did it hurt so bad?

Lifting her head high, she forced her Jell-O-like legs to cross the threshold, but then jumped when the door slammed closed behind her.

New tears raced down her face; she'd just made the biggest mistake of her life.

Back at the wedding…

Chapter 26

"Q!" Sterling shouted, and stormed toward his startled brother. "There you are. I've been looking all over the place for you."

"Well then, mission accomplished, dear bro." Quentin made a mock bow and then winked over at Alyssa. "If I'm not careful, one of these days they're going to implant a LoJack device under my skin and I'll never be able to sneak off with you again."

To her surprise, an uncharacteristic giggle tumbled from her lips. It was what other women did whenever they were around Quentin—not that she was a woman, yet. But soon, she promised herself, she would be.

Belatedly, Sterling noticed the starry-eyed

teenager. Suspicion narrowed his gaze as his eyes ping-ponged between the two. "Am I interrupting something?"

Q took one look at his brother's face and launched one eyebrow high along his forehead. "Certainly not what you're thinking."

Sterling cleared his throat while looking both guilty and embarrassed.

Alyssa wasn't sure she followed the conversation.

"I was simply filling little *Alyssa* in on how our wonderful brother Jonas has, once again, found himself ready to walk the plank to the abyss of happily-ever after."

Sterling's gaze fell to the empty champagne glass in his brother's hand. "How many of those have you had?"

"Not nearly enough." Q laughed. "But, hey, the night is still young." This time he clicked a wink at his older brother.

Sterling drew a deep breath in an obvious effort to remain calm. "Dad wants to see you. He's in his library." He glanced at his watch. "When you're done, Jonas wants to see you."

"Well, I guess I shouldn't keep them waiting," Q said, marching away.

Disappointed, Alyssa's shoulders slumped at having been so quickly forgotten. Then, as if he'd heard her thoughts, Q stopped and turned with a magnanimous smile.

"Oh, but I haven't finished telling poor little Alice the story."

Alice again.

Once again, Sterling's gaze shifted to the shy tomboy.

"Don't worry." Q smiled. "I was real careful to omit the racy parts. Perhaps you could finish for me?"

Horror rippled across the older Hinton's face like he wasn't quite used to talking to someone so young.

"Don't worry," Q continued, "she won't bite." He made a silent toast with his empty champagne glass and stalked off.

Alyssa smiled dreamily after her future husband until he disappeared into the house. A sigh she didn't even realize she was holding exploded from her chest.

Sterling chuckled.

Embarrassed, Alyssa's face heated to the point her cheeks felt like they were on fire.

"I've seen that look before," Sterling said, with an air of superiority that irked Alyssa. She didn't like for a moment that she'd given her emotions away to a man who would undoubtedly feel it was his duty to give her some type of speech.

"Don't worry," he covered, "your secret is safe with me."

Unable to hide her surprise, Alyssa eyed him with wary and cautious eyes.

"What?" he asked innocently enough. "I know what it's like to have a crush."

It took everything she had to protest and proclaim what she felt for Quentin was stronger than any playground crush. Q was her destiny.

"Or maybe I should say what it feels like to be in love?"

Alyssa experienced another bolt of surprise. Somehow the man was truly reading her thoughts.

Sterling smiled and for a brief moment, his handsome good looks rivaled his younger brother and she was stunned by how it sent her heart aflutter.

"I better get back to my room," she said, and turned toward the servants' quarters.

"You don't want to hear the rest of the story?"

Surprised, she stopped in her tracks. "You don't mind telling me?"

"Well, I'm sure I'm not as colorful a storyteller as Q...but if you really want to know."

Alyssa faced him again to judge whether he was being sincere or just being charitable.

"Where did you guys leave off?"

She hesitated; but when she realized that he was being sincere, she approached. "Jonas kicked Ms. Wright out of his condo after she tried to break things off."

"Well that is the PC version of things." He chuckled.

Alyssa frowned and Sterling cleared his throat.

"Well, let's just say that Jonas refused to speak to Toni after that...."

Chapter 27

Toni hadn't slept in two weeks.

As a result, her job performance suffered to the point she was failing to drum up the necessary clients she needed to stay afloat and frankly, she didn't care. She lost seven pounds on her already svelte frame, but food held no interest for her and neither did the fresh batch of men who passed her their numbers in restaurants, bars and even gas stations. All she could think about 24/7 was how much she missed Jonas.

Something was seriously wrong with her.

Admit it: you're in love with him.

The first few times those words floated across her head, she'd laughed. Laughed hard.

Fourteen days later, she wasn't laughing anymore.

A steady stream of questions raced across her head. Where was he now? Was he still angry about that night? If she called, would he talk to her?

This wasn't how it usually worked.

The routine was to pick out a new sexual partner, have some fun for a month, maybe two, break things off before either one got too serious and then cast her line back into the sea for another big fish.

Not this time.

She wanted the fish she'd just thrown away back.

Thinking about Jonas's stonelike features when he'd held open the door, it was clear there was no going back.

The realization made her chest ache.

In the past two weeks Toni had picked up the phone more times than she cared to admit. She'd dialed Jonas's number and like a silly teenager, hung up when he'd answered the line.

The shenanigans went on until the last time she'd called his personal numbers, she learned they'd all been changed.

A voice inside her head told her not to be too proud to beg and to march over to his office and throw herself at his mercy.

It was stupid.

So why did she drive to his office? It was point-less anyway. Hinton Enterprises' headquarters had packed up and moved back to South Carolina.

Now what?

Also in the past two weeks, she'd avoided calls from her girlfriends. Judging by the growing frantic messages on her answer machine, the tight sisterhood was on the verge of staging an intervention. Finally one evening, she picked up her ringing phone, determined to lie her way into forgiveness.

"I'm fine. I'm fine," she lied to Maria. "I've just been busy at the office."

Maria didn't believe a word. "You know, you don't always have to wear a damn Superwoman cape," she rebuffed. "I'm your girl. You can lean on my shoulders. Lord knows I've worn your shoulders out a time or two."

"C'mon." Toni tried her best to downplay her devastation. "It's nothing like that. Hell, I didn't even know him that well or that long. I'm good."

Maria grew quiet and Toni couldn't help but feel condemned by her sudden silence.

"I mean, sure, the sex was great." Actually, it was fantastic. "But you know me. I bore easy. It was time to move on."

"Still using the 'It's not you, it's me' speech?"

Another painful ache throbbed in her chest. "Hey, there's nothing wrong with sticking to what works."

"Whatever, girl. I'm not judging you."

"Yes, you are," Toni snapped before she had a chance to block the accusation from bursting from her lips. "You think I'm losing it," she continued uncensored. "You think I'm finally getting what's coming to me after years of thinking 'I don't need anybody.'" She sucked in a deep breath but then choked on a sob. "Well, it's true. I don't need any-body." She bolted to her feet and paced the familiar path before her bed. "Love, marriage, children. That's all women bitch about. Like being some man's property is the answer to our lives. Well, it's not. There's not a damn thing a man can do for me that I can't do for myself!"

Silence greeted her sudden tirade.

Toni squeezed her eyes shut and braced herself for the tidal wave of regret. When it hit, every limb in her body trembled and quaked. What was wrong with her? She usually had better control of her emotions than this.

Then again, it wasn't every day she'd thrown away a chance of a lifetime. A chance for real love.

Maria finally found her voice. "Maybe I should come out and visit you for a while? You know. Hang out like we used to."

Toni collapsed onto the edge of the bed, this time unable to prevent a low rumble of laughter from falling from her lips. "No. That's not necessary. I'm all right. We're all entitled to one hysterical outburst in life, right?"

Maria didn't answer. Probably was too afraid to.

"I better go," Toni said, wanting to get off the phone before another rant could take them both unawares. "I'll call you tomorrow."

"Promise?"

"Of course. I just have a lot to get done tonight," she lied. Tears trickled down her face as she ended the call. By the time she disconnected, her tears had transformed into a rushing river.

"I'm not in love with him. I'm not," she shouted into the empty room. But even the walls called her a liar.

"I'm not settling!" Nora Gibson snapped, leaning back in her chair and folding her slender arms to glare at her former bosses, her ex-lover and their team of attorneys.

Toni exhaled a long breath, wishing that she could somehow disappear underneath the table. Nothing she said would deter her client and after watching William Bassett's "The Best of Nora" home movies, Toni was almost willing to write her client a check from her own personal account to get her to go away.

At least Nora's ex-colleagues and girlfriends, who'd also filed suits, quietly dropped their claims and pulled a Houdini when Toni informed them of Mr. Bassett's home movies.

But not Nora.

The woman was unshakable and determined to win a big money payday. "Those tapes don't prove anything," Nora insisted, and then slapped on a smile. "I did those things in order to remain in good standing with this company."

"My client is correct," Toni informed the men in black across the table. The usual suspects were all there…except for Jonas. She sort of hoped he would be. "We acknowledge that Ms. Gibson had engaged in sexual acts with William Bassett. Our suit clearly states she felt pressure to participate and cultivate his wild fantasies."

Where in the hell did she pull that rabbit from?

"Ah, c'mon, B-pie," Willy crooned, winking at his ex-lover from across the table. "You know most of these games were your idea."

"B-pie?" Toni asked.

Willy's face lit up. "Yeah. It's sort of my pet name for the best damn *blackberry* pie this side of the Mississippi."

Toni gasped as the rest of the men in the room groaned. Suddenly feeling a little more confident in the case, Toni turned her gaze toward her opponent. "Brian, do you really want a jury to meet this man?"

Brian cast a calculating glance at Willy Bassett. He was seeing what she was seeing. A loud, aging playboy who would slip his head through a noose if there was a single woman in the jury box.

Even Marcel and Solomon looked nervous.

"I need a moment to confer with my clients," Brian finally said, standing from his chair and fiddling with the buttons on his suit.

Marcel and Solomon stood likewise.

Toni glanced at Nora, sensing at long last that a settlement was on the horizon. "Sure. You boys take all the time you need."

A train of black suits marched out of the conference room. The only man who refused to budge was Willy Bassett. His wide devil-may-care grin disturbed her. Did the other men purposely leave them in a den with a starving lion?

"That tape got me thinking about old times,

B-pie." Willy reached into his jacket and removed a fat Cuban cigar. "Remember the time we played Lewinsky right here in this room?"

Nora blushed.

Toni blinked and bolted back from the desk, disgusted by the image of what might have happened on this very desk.

"Let's wait in the break room down the hall?" Toni suggested, standing. For all she knew the walls were soundproof and no one would be able to hear them scream.

Nora looked like she might protest and Toni quickly snatched her client by the arm, more than ready to drag Nora out of the conference room by her hair if she had to.

As the two women made their escape into the hallway, Toni breathed a sigh of relief. "That man needs to be in a cage."

Nora chuckled. "He has one of those in his house for when he plays zoo-monkey."

"You're kidding me," Toni said.

Nora shrugged. "Actually. It's sort of fun."

Toni stopped walking and stared. "I'm going to forget you said that." She started walking again. "I wonder why Mr. Hinton didn't join us?" she asked as casually as she could. Despite Nora's unemployment, she still seemed to know most of the inner workings of T&B.

"Oh, Marcel and Solomon bought him out. Guess he decided he didn't want to be in the entertainment business, after all. Frankly, I think he's finally gotten it through his thick skull that Ophelia was never going to crawl back to him."

Toni's heart plummeted and knocked around somewhere in her knees. She had forgotten all about Ophelia Bassett and the real reason Jonas had moved to Atlanta in the first place. How in the hell did she manage that?

Stupid. Stupid. Stupid.

Somehow she managed to keep her self-disgust from cracking her professional calm, but what raged inside of her was another story altogether.

"Speaking of the devil," Nora said as they stepped into the break room. "Good morning, Ophelia."

Toni glanced up then felt the air rush out of her lungs when recognition surged through her brain.

Chapter 28

Ophelia was more beautiful than Toni had imagined. And no matter what she did, she couldn't stop her jealous gaze from desperately seeking a flaw to verify that she was, indeed, human. She couldn't find one.

Damn it.

"Hello." Ophelia smiled, but then her finger waved like a baton between them. "Haven't we met before?"

Nora's curious gaze shifted to her attorney.

"You're not an employee here, are you?"

"She's my attorney, Ms. Toni Wright," Nora announced. "She's about to make me a rich woman."

Ophelia's friendly demeanor shifted. "Toni?"

Without warning, the first words out of Toni's mouth took everyone in the room by surprise. "I used to date Jonas Hinton."

The silence that stretched between the three women lasted so long, Toni worried that she had temporarily gone deaf. However, it was Nora who was the first to find her tongue.

"Come again?"

Toni forced a smile on her lips and calmly turned toward her client. "Would you give us a few minutes?"

The look on Nora's face clearly said *hell, no,* which caused Toni to quickly add, "Please."

After drawing in a couple of deep breaths and tossing a pointed look at Mrs. Bassett, Nora finally caved. "A few minutes," she emphasized. "And then we need to talk about conflicts of interest."

Toni nodded and then waited patiently for Nora to exit the room. "Mind if I close the door?"

Ophelia hesitated, but then acquiesced with a slight nod.

The door closed with a soft click and when Toni turned to face Jonas's ex, she honestly didn't know what she was going to say until it tumbled out of her mouth. "What I should have said was that I'm in love with Jonas Hinton, and though I don't want to face it, I believe there's a part of him that is still in love with you."

Ophelia's gaze dropped like a stone. "I don't know what to tell you about that." Her shoulders tugged slightly. "Only that it's over between us. It has been for some time."

"And yet, he bought an interest in your husband's company only to be near you."

Ophelia's head snapped back up. "Did he tell you that?"

"He didn't need to," Toni said, pulling out a chair. "Just like he didn't need to tell you." She sat down and made herself comfortable.

"Or my husband," Ophelia tossed in, drawing out her own chair. After a few wild heartbeats the silence grew awkward, but then Ophelia confessed, "Jonas told Solomon about you."

Toni lifted her chin, but she couldn't mask her surprise.

A pleased smile touched Ophelia's lips. "He may have bought his way into T&B Entertainment for me, but he most certainly sold it because of you."

An unexpected wave of relief washed over Toni, but it quickly receded when her old fear returned.

"You said you loved him...so what happened?"

Toni blinked. She did admit that, didn't she? What the hell was she thinking? Regardless, she couldn't get herself to take the words back. Instead, she continued with her confession. "I don't want to love him. Love is...tricky. Messy. Temporary."

Ophelia's expression twisted. "You don't really believe that, do you?"

"Don't you?" Toni clamped her mouth shut and mentally berated herself for the careless admission.

"No. I don't," the golden beauty answered. "Love

is the most beautiful gift you can give or receive from a person. Love is life. And if you miss love, you miss life."

Despite being touched and even stirred by the short speech, Toni couldn't banish her mother's voice from her head.

Love is a woman's greatest downfall.

Ophelia leaned across the table and covered Toni's hand. "I certainly can't tell you what to do and I don't know the details of what's happened between you two, but walking away from love doesn't seem to have made you too happy. But I can guarantee you if you run toward it—your heart— your life will only be rewarded. Love in the moment and the energy of the moment."

Tears burned the back of Toni's eyes and she sandwiched Ophelia's hand.

"It's never too late," Ophelia added. "Trust me. I know. If you love him, go get him."

When Toni emerged from the break room, she was in a rush to reach a settlement with the partners of T&B so she could get home and develop a plan to win her man back. However, her mind was wiped clean when she opened the door to the conference room and found Nora and Willy making out on top of the conference table.

Nora's eyes bulged as she made a lame attempt to cover her breast and scramble off the table.

A sweating Uncle Willy only smiled and said, "Come on in. The more the merrier!"

"What?" Nora popped him over the head.

Behind Toni, Solomon and Marcel approached and apparently became just as speechless.

"I guess this means I won't be getting a settlement?" Nora inquired, red-faced.

"Aw. Don't worry, B-pie," Uncle Willy gushed. "You still have me."

When it comes to women, keep your emotions out of it, Jonas reminded himself as he clinked glasses with Patsy Nelson.

"I have to admit, I was a little surprised to hear from you today." She glanced around Silk, her favorite Japanese restaurant, and then beamed her smile back at him. "It's not my birthday so what's the special occasion?"

"No special occasion," Jonas assured. "After what happened at Club Secrets I figured I should make it up to you."

A saucy smile slithered across Patsy's face while her eyes lit with renewed interest. "Does this mean you'll be coming back to my place after dinner?"

A soft rumble of laughter rolled inside Jonas's chest. "No. That won't be happening."

Patsy's face fell with disappointment.

"I was hoping you would come back to *my* place," he said, watching her eyes reignite.

"It's about time you came back to your senses," she gloated, sipped her champagne and encouraged him to, "Eat up. You're going to need the energy."

* * *

After dinner, Jonas and Patsy started making out as soon as the door slid closed in the lobby of his penthouse building. Patsy's lips were nice, even pleasant, but they failed to heat his blood or quicken his heart rate the way...

Keep your emotions out of it.

He tried his best to recreate the sparks he'd shared with Toni, but to no avail. The more he deepened the kiss, the emptier he felt.

Seconds later, the elevator delivered them to his floor. Patsy continued to kiss and tear at his clothes while he wrestled to reach for his keys.

"I'm going to give you a night you'll never forget," she promised, between gentle pecks while he fiddled with the door.

Upon opening it, the couple tumbled into the condominium laughing, kissing and pulling at each other's clothes.

Don't think. Keep your heart out of it, Jonas recited. He could do this. He had to do it in order to purge Toni from his mind and body.

But it wasn't working.

Patsy broke the kiss to stare curiously up at him. "Is something wrong?"

Jonas coughed and cleared his throat. "No. No. Everything is fine." He pulled her close and tried kissing her again. Again, nothing.

Patsy didn't quiver like Toni.

She didn't sigh like Toni.

And her strong perfume was nothing like the soft floral scent of… *Stop it.*

He deepened the kiss, but soon realized that it was hopeless. "I'm sorry, Patsy," he said, breaking away from her. "I can't do this."

Patsy heaved a frustrated sigh, her beautiful face now a mask of frustration and irritation. "Let me guess. You're in love with another woman."

Toni entered the lobby of Jonas's building wearing a slick, silver raincoat, a matching pair of silver pumps and a smile. Underneath: she was stark naked. She was surprised that no one was manning the desk, but she still remembered Jonas's elevator code and went straight up.

She didn't have much of a plan. Only to show up, say she was sorry and open her coat. Past experience told her this would be enough to get back in the good graces of any man. As soon as that thought drifted across her brain, a voice in the back of her head reminded her that Jonas was no ordinary man.

He could be moody.

Stubborn.

And even carry grudges too long.

"Don't think about that now," she coached herself. Her plan *had* to work. She wanted him back. She needed him.

Jonas felt like a complete ass. "I'm sorry, Patsy. Really, I am."

Patsy tried to remain angry with him, but it just wasn't working. She exhaled a long sigh and gave a careless shrug. "It's all right. I should have known this night was too good to be true."

She headed back toward the door while Jonas followed silently behind her. When she crossed the threshold, she turned a final time to face him. "I think you should get a new attorney."

Jonas opened his mouth to protest but she placed a silencing finger against his lips. "I insist." She smiled. "Whoever she is, I hope she deserves you." Leaning up on her toes, Patsy kissed him goodbye.

A soft gasp caught their attention.

Jonas looked up and felt his heart lurch. "Toni." Before he could finish whispering her name, she was gone.

Chapter 29

The Carolina Panthers' first game of the season against the Atlanta Falcons in Charlotte was a tragedy to behold. The Hinton men moaned and groaned inside Jonas's box seats like they were all experiencing one gigantic bellyache. By halftime, the score was 13-3 with the Falcons posting 159 rushing yards.

"I sure hope this isn't an indication of how the whole season will pan out," Q said, tossing back the rest of his beer. "If so, you're looking at one looong season."

Jonas viewed everything that was being played out on the field as an omen. This would be how the year would turn out, he decided. Why would this season be any different than the past three months since he'd last seen Toni?

The stricken look on her face was something he couldn't banish from his thoughts or his dreams. Her eyes had been bright with unshed tears—her full lips trembled at the sight of him with Patsy.

At the time, pride forbade him to give chase; but now, he was certain he'd made yet another colossal mistake. His mind filled with so many wouldas, couldas, shouldas that it was impossible to think of anything else.

"Maybe you should look into replacing the coach," Sterling commented after watching the team fail to execute yet another play. "I know Fox is a good man and all, but…"

Jonas just gave a stubborn shake of his head and went back to nursing his ginger ale. This time around, he refused to drown his sorrow with alcohol. He didn't want to forget any of his time with Toni. He treasured every memory. The good *and* the bad.

It also meant that he suffered through three months of his younger brothers campaigning to cheer him up. Q even went so far as to donate his personal black book with all his top play toys highlighted.

Sterling tried to exercise him to death, but no amount of hiking, biking or mountain climbing was going to purge Toni out of his system.

Why didn't he chase after her that night?

The rest of the game passed as a blur. When the final score of 20-6 was posted, the Hinton brothers stood and looked as if they'd survived the funeral service of a close relative.

After a quick meal, Jonas still didn't want to talk

about replacing coaches or team players. He did, however, wonder endlessly about what Toni was doing at this moment—and who she was doing it with.

He wasn't a fool. A woman like Toni wouldn't be alone for long. He experienced another painful squeeze in his chest. When he went to rub the ache away, it caught his brother's attention.

"I wish you would go see a doctor about that," Sterling said with real concern. "Chest pains are nothing to play with."

"I will. I will," Jonas promised for like the umpteenth time in the past month.

"Please. There's nothing wrong with him." Q tossed his knife and fork onto his half-eaten Porterhouse steak. "Just call the girl already!"

Jonas's jaw instantly hardened as he gave Q a warning glare.

However, Quentin just waved the warning off and even rolled his eyes skyward. "Don't give me that look. I'm tired of watching you mope around. Call her."

"Q." Sterling's voice also held a note of warning.

"What? Are you going to pretend that you don't know what's going on, too? Or maybe you'll just advise him to purchase the girl's law practice so he can be close to her?"

Sterling's face darkened from anger or embarrassment, Q didn't know which and he didn't care. All he knew was this madness must end. "Call her," he said again. "Please. I'll do anything if you'd just call. Hell, I'll even get a job. Call her."

Surprise blanketed the brothers' faces.

"For how long?" Sterling inquired.

"I don't know—a month."

"A year," Sterling negotiated.

"Six months," Q countered.

Sterling turned to Jonas. "Call her."

"What? I'm not calling her." He shifted in his chair. "I can't." He wanted to call. "It's too late."

"Then just call and ask her for the time," Sterling urged. "We may never have another opportunity to get Q to actually draw a paycheck again."

"Amen," Q quipped.

"As tempting an offer as that may be... What are you doing?"

Sterling lifted his hips and scooped out his cell phone. "I know I still have her number listed in my cell." He scrolled through the electronic phone book.

"Sterling—"

"Ah, here it is." He handed over the phone. "Just hit Send."

"I'm not calling."

"You *are* calling or we're going to have one hell of a fight right here in this restaurant," he promised.

Q looked pleased with himself.

Despite being in pretty good shape, Jonas knew Sterling, with his ungodly amount of hours in the gym, could take him. Jonas took the phone. "What am I going to say?"

"I'm no rocket scientist," Q jumped in. "But most people usually go with a classic like 'hello.'"

"You look a little too smug for someone who's going to have to hold down a *j-o-b* for six months."

"You haven't made the call yet."

He had him there. Jonas looked down at the razor-thin phone and stared at Toni's name across the screen. Suddenly his heart began to race, and blood roared in his ears, causing him to feel light-headed. Maybe he was having a heart attack.

"Call her," both brothers chanted in unison.

Jonas drew a deep breath, hit the send button and placed the phone against his ear. His heart continued to accelerate as he listened to the line ring.

"Hello," a man answered.

Jonas's voice seized in his throat.

"Hello," the man said again.

"Yes, may I speak to Toni?"

"She's, um, in the bathroom at the moment. Can I take a message?"

Jonas shook his head. "No. No message." He quickly disconnected the call and tossed the phone back at Sterling. "Satisfied?" He held up a hand and flagged down their waitress. "Scotch on the rocks—and make it a double."

"Was that my phone?" Toni asked, carrying a box of her toiletries into the living room.

"It was," Isaiah said, returning the cordless to its cradle. He turned and reclaimed the box he'd set down on the table. "Guy didn't want to leave a message."

Toni's heart quickened, but before she could question Brooklyn's husband further, he was out the door and headed toward the moving van. She was lucky that Brooklyn and her husband were back in town for the week and could help her move.

"Are you sure you want to move back to California?" Brooklyn asked. "You haven't even been here six months."

"I should have never come back," Toni said, moving over to the phone to screen the caller ID. "I'm lucky that Kaplan, Grey & Kaplan wants me back."

"So you're giving up on your own firm?"

"For now. Way too much headache. And now that I'm…well, you know. I need something with a little less stress." She hit the button to see the last caller. Sterling Hinton.

Toni blinked in surprise. Her curiosity churned out a million possibilities for the call. She picked up the phone and started to push the talk button to redial the number, but then stopped.

For three months, she had been trying to forget Jonas Hinton. Hands down, it had been one of the hardest things she had ever tried to do. And here it was, one call and she was ready to run back to his world. Hell, he wasn't even Jonas. It was his brother.

What did they think, that they could just keep passing her around like some kind of serving tray? Who knows, maybe she'd get the trifecta and Quentin would start calling.

"Toni?" Brooklyn broke through her troubled thoughts. "Where did you go?" She laughed and slid another strip of tape across another box.

"Oh, I'm sorry. What did you say?" She set the phone back down and returned to packing.

"I asked whether you thought about moving to Texas? I know I'd love it if you were there in Austin. If would be like old times. You and me—"

"And the kids," Toni added. She didn't mean for the words to have such a biting edge, but she knew the drill. Married girlfriends weren't the same as single girlfriends. Their conversations were or would always turn into subjects about their husbands and kids. "Oh, such and such did the funniest thing today" or "guess what my husband did today."

Then again, retuning to California meant Botox parties, getting the pointers about the latest starvation diet and constantly having your body image accosted. And that would be within the first five minutes at Maria's apartment.

"I don't know, Brooklyn." She sighed. "I just know this place holds too many memories for me."

Sighing, Brooklyn laid down the box tape. "Toni, why don't you just call him?"

Toni started to ask, "call who?" but one look into Brooklyn's serious face, and she knew playing dumb wasn't going to work. "There's nothing to say. It's over."

"Okay. Where is the next box?" Isaiah asked, stomping back into the house.

"All the boxes in the kitchen are marked and ready to go," Toni informed him.

Isaiah slapped his hands together and headed toward the kitchen.

Brooklyn waited until he was out of earshot

before returning to the subject at hand. "Come on, Toni. You're miserable. I've never seen you like this."

"I'm fine," she lied.

Brooklyn laughed.

"What's so funny?"

"I remember a time when you were trying to get me to call Isaiah when we broke up. I kept telling you I was fine when I was anything but." She met Toni's gaze. "I felt like I was dying inside. Slowly but surely."

Toni was the first to look away. That was exactly how she felt.

"After what happened between me and Evan… and Macy, I was positive that marriage wasn't for me. I didn't want to depend on another man. Love *isn't* a woman's greatest downfall. It's the inability to love." Brooklyn stood up and walked over to her best friend. "Call him."

After dinner, the Hinton brothers returned home to Jonas's South Carolina condo. Luckily, Sterling was the designated driver because once Jonas started drinking, he seemed unable to stop. At one point when Jonas was really blitzed, he'd grabbed Sterling by his head and spoke with such pain that it nearly tore Sterling's heart in two.

"I love her. A million times more than what's-her-face."

In a couple hours, Jonas had covered a gamut of emotions. One minute he was laughing and the next he would brood into his drink. Sterling considered himself lucky not to have crossed paths with a woman who could do this to him.

Real lucky.

Once they arrived at Jonas's, Sterling and Q each grabbed an arm and a leg and carried their brother to his bedroom.

"See. This is why I say keep your emotions out of it when dealing with women," Q commented after they had gotten Jonas into bed.

Sterling stared down at their older brother sleeping like a baby. "Yeah. I just wish there was something we could do for him."

The younger brothers went back out of the room and closed the door.

"Well, I'm going out," Q announced.

"It's two in the morning," Sterling said.

"That may be, but I'm not going to be like you two losers. I need something soft and warm to curl up to tonight." He bolted toward the stairs. "Don't wait up."

"Don't forget about your agreement. First thing tomorrow, you need to be looking for a job."

"Yeah. Yeah. Yeah." Q raced out the front door.

Shaking his head, Sterling felt his cell phone vibrate against his leg. Who on earth could be calling him this late?

He scooped the phone out of his pocket and froze. It was Toni Wright.

Chapter 30

Jonas woke with a massive hangover. When bits and pieces of what happened the night before floated back to the forefront, he groaned and moaned over his behavior—and the fact he'd done it in front of his brothers. The most humiliating part had to be when he stood up and changed the words to Barry Manilow's song "Mandy" to "Toni."

Why did he even know the lyrics to that song?

After a quick shower and a change, Jonas rushed from the house before either of his brothers had a chance to corner him and poke fun at what happened last night.

And he certainly didn't want to remember the man's voice who'd answered Toni's phone. Jonas wasn't dumb. A relationship had to have progressed rather well for a man to have permission to answer a woman's phone.

It was all the evidence he needed to prove that Toni had moved on.

Jumping on the back of his Harley, Jonas blinked in surprise at a brief handwritten note taped on his bike. *Meet me at the skybox—Sterling.*

What the hell? He pulled the note off and balled it up. Leave it to Sterling to anticipate his first move—an annoying habit of his.

Drawing a deep breath, Jonas glanced at his watch and started his bike. He may as well head over to the stadium; he certainly didn't feel up to going into the office today. A light drizzle dotted his wind visor as he joined the morning traffic. Forty-five minutes later, he arrived at the stadium's skybox, but judging how the light rain had turned into a torrential downpour, he knew practice would be cancelled. Still, he dropped into one of the leather chairs and kicked back.

Maybe he needed to go away somewhere where he could clear his mind. A vacation.

A long vacation.

He certainly couldn't go back to the Caribbean. The island would only remind him of Toni. Yet, he wanted to be reminded. He wanted to remember what it felt like caressing her skin, kissing her mouth and plunging himself as deep as he could inside of her.

A sad laugh escaped his lips, but then he sobered and drew a deep breath. Hell, even now he could recall the sweet smell of lavender that always clung to Toni's skin.

Was he going mad?

"A penny for your thoughts."

Jonas's eyes snapped open, but he couldn't turn around.

Toni's awkward laugh tumbled behind him. "That line never works with you."

He drew a deep breath, but still didn't turn around. "What are you doing here?"

"Haven't you heard? I'm a glutton for punishment." The room fell silent, and then, "I talked with Sterling. He brought me here."

Jonas vowed to kill his brother.

"Aren't you going to turn around?"

Jonas didn't know if he should. He didn't trust himself to keep it together once he saw her. He was afraid he would run to her and fall to his knees. Undoubtedly, he would beg and promise her the world if she would just take him back.

The soft rustle of fabric caught his attention and he listened as her light footsteps approached from behind. Seconds later, lavender invaded Jonas's senses and he clutched the sides of the leather chair, hoping it would aid him to keep it together.

"I'm sorry," she whispered so softly that he barely heard her. "In the Caribbean," she went on. "When you told me you loved me...I got scared. You see, I was falling in love with you, too, and...well, I've always made it a rule to get out before emotions come into play."

Jonas remained silent as his hands tightened on the chair.

"Only this time, I didn't get out in time," she added. "My parents...didn't die in a car accident," she said softly. "My father was a very abusive man."

Jonas tensed.

"He would beat my mother often. For years, no matter what he did, my mother wouldn't leave him. She always said that she couldn't leave because she loved him." Toni sniffed and struggled to continue. "One of the things my mother ingrained in me was: love was a woman's greatest downfall. I believed her. When she finally grew tired of the beatings, we packed up our things and moved into a women's shelter in Atlanta. When my father came home from work and discovered we were gone, he came looking for us. He shot my mother and then turned the gun on himself."

Tears streaked down Jonas's eyes as he listened.

"All these years, I've been afraid to fall in love. Afraid of what it would do to me. But it happened anyway. I miss you." She placed a hand on his shoulder. "I love you, Jonas."

Her touch effectively destroyed his wall of resistance and he reached up to cover her hand with his own. "I love you, too."

Toni walked around the leather chair to face him. Once again, she wore the same silver raincoat. To look at her was to look at love and Jonas knew at that moment he wanted to spend the rest of his life waking up and lying down with this woman.

"Marry me." The words were out of his mouth before he knew it. And there was nothing on earth that could describe the joy he felt when he watched her eyes fill with joyous tears.

"You stole the words right out of my mouth." She laughed.

Jonas jumped to his feet and pulled her close. Their lips connected and a bolt of electricity shot through them. "I love you, Toni," he murmured once he came up for air. "I've felt like the walking dead these past three months. You are my heart. My soul. Never leave me again. Promise."

"I promise," she groaned, and then pressed her lips against his again. Arching gently against him, an old familiar ache throbbed within her. Her sexual hunger only intensified when she felt his desire harden and press against her pelvis.

Desire swirled like a tornado through her veins as she slipped her hands up his broad back. She stroked its hard planes and ardently wished she could do away with his clothes. Yet, there was one more thing she had to do.

"Baby." Her fevered whisper trembled. "There's something I have to tell you."

Jonas broke away with a frown already touching his face. "If it's about you seeing someone else during these last few months." He swallowed. "It's okay. It's in the past. You're mine now. We're together."

Confusion twisted Toni's expression. "I haven't been seeing anyone since we've broken up."

Jonas failed to cover his surprise and his pleasure. "When I called yesterday, a man—"

Toni shook her head. "Isaiah answered the phone."

The name didn't ring any bells so he waited for an explanation.

"Isaiah is my best friend's husband. They were helping me pack yesterday."

Another wave of relief hit, but then, "Pack? Where are you going?"

Toni's gaze dropped to the wide span of his chest. "I was moving back to California. I was trying to run away from the pain of losing you."

Jonas cupped the bottom of her chin and tilted it up. "Well, you don't have to run any farther. You're right where you belong." His mouth descended again and the passion he unleashed left her swaying in his arms.

She still hadn't told him yet.

"J-Jonas," she managed to say during his torrential love storm. "There is still something I have to tell you, baby."

"Can it wait?" His hands reached to undo the belt of her coat. "I want you. I need you right now."

Her sash fell open.

"But—"

Jonas peeled the coat from her shoulders.

"It's important."

When the coat hit the floor, Jonas glanced down and froze. Toni's beautiful, nude body still had the power to excite and ignite his passion; but there was no mistaking the small bump of her belly. "Baby…"

Toni pressed her warm, soft hand against his stubbled cheek. "The first two months I think I was in denial. And then I didn't want to trap you into—"

Jonas silenced her with a kiss. He poured everything he had into it and he was rewarded when she did the same. Soon, the couple tasted the salt of each other's tears and it only made their joining that much sweeter—that much hungrier—that much more satisfying.

And it would be so, Jonas vowed, for the rest of their lives.

Epilogue

Alyssa sighed when Sterling finally finished the story. It wrapped with a happy ending—just the way she liked them. Now, here she was at the center of what would undoubtedly be dubbed a fairy-tale wedding…and she had to stay in her room.

"Fifteen minutes to showtime." The wedding planner rushed around alerting the wedding party. "Everyone take their places."

Sterling smiled and stood up straight. "I guess that means me, too." His gaze raked over her attire: blue jeans, Mary J. Blige T-shirt and a pair of Reeboks that had seen better days. "I know I'm long past being hip. Well, I was never what you would call hip…but is that what you're wearing to the wedding?"

Alyssa dropped her head and couldn't help but poke out her bottom lip. "I can't go. Dad said that I would just be in the way."

Sterling chuckled and then placed a comforting arm around her shoulders. "Nonsense." He looked her over again. "It just so happens that I require a date for this evening. How fast can you change clothes?"

Hope bloomed in Alyssa's heart. "But Daddy said—"

"I'll have a talk with Alfred. I'm sure I can get him to change his mind."

"Do you really think so?"

Sterling's chest swelled with confidence. "I'm a pretty persuasive guy. It's served me well in business."

"Yeah, but—"

"Trust me."

He winked and again Alyssa was charmed by his uncharacteristic playful side. "Okay," she said, backing away. "I'll go change." She turned and raced off to her room. The only dress she had in her closet suitable for a wedding was the frilly number her father had bought her for Easter. She frowned at the excessive lace, but quickly showered and shimmied into the dress in what had to be an Olympic record.

A couple of brush strokes through her hair, a ribbon and she was out the door. As she rushed to grab one of the white, wooden lawn chairs she took in the final staging for the ceremony and felt as if she had been cast into a glorious dream. White and pink flowers were strewn as far as the eye could see while a live orchestra played as if they were introducing her to the crowd.

No sooner had she found a seat on the groom's side, did someone hand her a folded letter. She suspected it was from her father before she even opened it.

And she was right. *Be on your* best *behavior—Dad.*

Alyssa smiled and folded the letter. Sterling had pulled off a miracle and she would be eternally grateful.

A handsome Jonas took his place before the preacher, looking happy *and* nervous. The processional music started up and everyone turned in their seats in time to see the first bridesmaid and groomsman march down the aisle.

Of course, Alyssa's heart didn't start pounding until Quentin appeared, escorting a blushing Maria. Alyssa pretended not to notice the subtle signs of the beautiful Latina flirting with her future husband. Q spotted Alyssa in the crowd and winked.

In that moment, if she had died, she would have left this world one of the happiest girls alive.

I will marry you one day, Quentin Dwayne Hinton. I will.

Sterling was the next Hinton to walk down the aisle. When he, too, spotted her in her silly Easter dress, he smiled and gave her the thumbs-up. She smiled and mouthed the words *thank you.*

The wedding march began and everyone rose to their feet when the bride marched down the aisle on the arm of her friend Isaiah Washington. She was six months pregnant and glowed like the sun. When everyone returned to their seats, they all waited in anticipation of the "I do's."

This time, neither the bride nor groom stopped the wedding. Precisely twenty minutes later, the minister introduced Mr. and Mrs. Hinton to the crowd.

The fairy-tale wedding wasn't over for Alyssa. To her surprise, Q offered his arm for her first dance. Being in his arms was like a dream come true and it took everything she had not to make a fool of herself.

"Ah, I still stand by my earlier assessment," he said. "One day, you *will* break men's hearts. I just pray I won't be one of them."

She was sure her entire body turned beet-red and it was a wonder that she didn't trip all over his feet.

However, when the song ended, Quentin disappeared to sweep another woman off her feet.

"May I?" Sterling asked.

"Yes, you may." Alyssa glided into his arms and soon discovered he was as good a dancer as his younger brother. "Thank you for talking my dad into letting me attend."

"Oh, think nothing of it. What else are friends for?"

She smiled, feeling for the first time that she was his friend and not just some servant's daughter. Alas, the dance ended too quickly and Sterling disappeared into the crowd, as well.

"My. My. My. Aren't you popular with the Hinton

men," an attractive woman in a stunning aqua-blue gown whispered. "If you were a little older, I'm willing to bet half the eligible women here would be plotting to scratch your eyes out."

Alyssa giggled, liking the idea of women being jealous of her. Especially those who think they actually had a chance with her man. "They're welcome to try," she whispered back.

It was the woman's turn to giggle. "I like you, little girl. You have spunk."

It wasn't spunk, Alyssa knew. She had a plan.

Author's Note

I wonder what little Alyssa has up her sleeves. Does she really think she has what it takes to lasso Quentin and drag him to the altar? Isn't she a little too young for him? Well, one thing's for sure, she has plenty of time to plot and scheme. Also, I want to give a special thanks to Ms. Patsy Nelson for being a Byrdwatcher contest winner and winning the chance to become a character in this book. As promised, you kissed Jonas Hinton. If you would like to join the Byrdwatcher family, please feel free to drop by my Web site: www.adriannebyrd.com

Hope to see you there.

Best of love,

Adrianne Byrd

Love can be sweeter the second time around...

USA TODAY Bestselling Author

KAYLA PERRIN

Midnight Dreams

Betrayed by her husband, Jade Alexander resolved never again to trust a man with her heart. But after meeting old flame Terrell Edmonds at a New Year's Eve party, Jade feels her resolve weakening— and her desire kindling.

Terrell had lost Jade by letting her marry the wrong man. Now he must convince her that together they can make all their New Year wishes come true...

"A fine storytelling talent."
—the *Toronto Star*

Available the first week of November
wherever books are sold.

ARABESQUE®

www.kimanipress.com

KPKP0251107

Sex changed everything...

Forbidden Temptation

ESSENCE BESTSELLING AUTHOR

Gwynne FORSTER

The morning after her sister's wedding, Ruby Lockhart finds herself in bed with her best friend, sexy ex-SEAL Luther Biggens. Luther's always been Ruby's rock...now he's her problem! She can't look at him without remembering the ways he pleasured her...or that she wants him to do it again.

THE LOCKHARTS

THREE WEDDINGS AND A REUNION
FOR FOUR SASSY SISTERS, ROMANCE CHANGES EVERYTHING!

*Available the first week of November
wherever books are sold.*

KIMANI
ROMANCE
™

www.kimanipress.com

KPGF0401107

Business takes on a new flavor...

SEX ON FLAMINGO *Beach*

Part of the Flamingo Beach series

Bestselling author

MARCIA KING-GAMBLE

Rowan James's plans to open a casino next door may cost
resort manager Emilie Woodward her job. So when he asks
her out, suspicion competes with sizzling attraction. What's
he after—a no-strings fling or a competitive advantage?

"Down and Out in Flamingo Beach showcases
Marcia King-Gamble's talent for accurately
portraying life in a small town."
—*Romantic Times BOOKreviews*

*Available the first week of November
wherever books are sold.*

KIMANI™
ROMANCE

www.kimanipress.com

Could they have a new beginning?

Pride
AND
Consequence

Favorite author

ALTONYA WASHINGTON

When devastating illness strikes him, Malik's pride causes him to walk out on his passionate life with Zakira. She is devastated but dedicates herself to their business. But when Malik returns fully recovered, Zakira is stunned... and still angry. Now Malik will need more than soul-searing kisses to win her trust again. He will have to make her believe in them...again.

Available the first week of November wherever books are sold.

KIMANI™
ROMANCE

www.kimanipress.com

KPAW0421107

The Knight family trilogy continues...

to love a
KNIGHT
WAYNE JORDAN

As Dr. Tamara Knight cares for gravely injured
Jared St. Clair, she's drawn to his rugged sensuality and
commanding strength. Despite his gruff exterior, she can't
stop herself from indulging in a passionate love affair with
him. But unbeknownst to Tamara, Jared was sent to save
her. Now protecting Tamara isn't just another mission for
Jared—it's all that matters!

"Mr. Jordan's writing simply captures his audience."
—*The Road to Romance*

*Available the first week of November
wherever books are sold.*

KIMANI™
ROMANCE

www.kimanipress.com

KPWJ0431107

A volume of heartwarming devotionals
that will nourish your soul...

NORMA DeSHIELDS BROWN

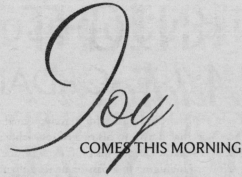

Joy

COMES THIS MORNING

Norma DeShields Brown's life suddenly changed
when her only son was tragically taken from her
by a senseless act. Consumed by grief, she began
an intimate journey that became
Joy Comes This Morning.

Filled with thoughtful devotions, Scripture readings
and words of encouragement, this powerful book
will guide you on a spiritual journey that will sustain
you throughout the years.

*Available the first week of November
wherever books are sold.*

www.kimanipress.com   KPNDB0351107

GET THE GENUINE LOVE
YOU DESERVE...

NATIONAL BESTSELLING AUTHOR
Vikki Johnson

Addicted to COUNTERFEIT LOVE

Many people in today's world are unable to recognize
what a genuine loving partnership should be and
often sabotage one when it does come along. In this
moving volume, Vikki Johnson offers memorable
words that will help readers identify destructive love
patterns and encourage them to demand the love
that they are entitled to.

Available the first week of October wherever books are sold.

NEW SPIRIT
™

www.kimanipress.com

KPVJ0381007